ALESSANDRO'S PRIZE

BY

HELEN BIANCHIN

MILLS
BOON

First published in Great Britain 2011
by Mills & Boon, an imprint of Harlequin (UK) Limited.
Large Print edition 2011
Harlequin (UK) Limited, Eton House,
18-24 Paradise Road, Richmond, Surrey TW9 1SR

© Helen Bianchin 2011

ISBN: 978 0 263 22234 0

Printed and bound in Great Britain
by CPI Antony Rowe, Chippenham, Wiltshire

ALESSANDRO'S
PRIZE

To my husband, Danilo,
and our children Lucia, Angelo and Peter.
With sincere thanks for your encouragement
and support through the years.

CHAPTER ONE

ALESSANDRO DEL MARCO eased the sleek black sports car to a halt in the parking bay reserved for guests adjacent to the magnificent villa built at the edge of Lake Como.

Owned by the late Giuseppe dalla Silvestri, the villa was now occupied by his widow, the elegant Sophia, whose efforts in the aid of children's charities was legend.

It had been Giuseppe, Alessandro reflected, who had taken Alessandro in as a wild young teenager abandoned to the streets of Milan by unfit parents. A boy who, by a combination of street smarts and cunning had managed to evade the government system, and who had quickly learnt to fend for himself among others of his kind.

Giuseppe had earned the teenager's reluctant trust, fashioned his edgy talent with electronics

from illegal to legal dealings, ensured comple-
tion of his education, and then employed him and
taught and honed his business skills. Then, when
he had been ready, he had backed him financially
into his own electronics firm.

A consortium now known as Del Marco
Industries. A successful empire, which afforded
Alessandro a luxurious villa in the hills overlooking Lake Como, an apartment in Milan, real
estate in several major capitals around the world,
a private jet, and a small fleet of expensive cars.

Then there were the women...*plural.* Beautiful,
captivating women who sought his company, his
bed...in return for the social status associated
with the man he had become.

None of whom succeeded in extending anything other than a temporary relationship lasting
mere weeks, a few months at most, despite their
various ploys to hold his attention.

Had he become jaded? Perhaps. Never bored,
but a little tired of the feminine gender who tried
so hard to please, acting out a part they imagined he sought. Beautiful, engaging arm candy,
socially acceptable, intelligent, visually perfect...
and merely players on the stage of life.

His youth had hardened him, created a wariness in order to deal with the ugliness of surviving on the streets. To be constantly on watch for an ill-intentioned demand and recognize if the hand in a pocket held a knife, a knuckle-duster about to maim, or merely coins.

To fight, and win by any means.

It had been Giuseppe who had patiently gifted his business acumen and time, but Sophia who had taught Alessandro social skills, guided and chided him with genuine affection.

During the initial few years, when in his late teens, any lingering doubts regarding his worthiness in an elevated society were very thoroughly dispensed with by the two people who had chosen to take him beneath their wing.

You are a young man among men, equal in every aspect that matters, Giuseppe had counselled. *Never forget where you came from...then measure the success you have achieved by your efforts.*

He owed them, despite their denial. Giuseppe had become the father he never knew. And Sophia—well, for her he would do anything she asked of him.

Such as this evening's dinner invitation to join a few guests to welcome Sophia's niece and god-daughter, Lily Parisi, from Sydney, Australia. A young woman he'd met many years ago as a teenager when she'd visited Sophia and Giuseppe with her parents.

A solemn girl with beautiful dark chocolate brown eyes and dark hair confined in a single plait. Who even at such a young age appeared delightfully unaware of the captivating quality of her smile or her zest for life.

She had changed, of course. He'd seen pho-tographic evidence of those changes, had the essence of some of her correspondence relayed to him over the ensuing years. He had learnt of her parents' accidental death, Lily's success in taking over the Parisi family restaurant, her en-gagement...only to be privy to Sophia's distress when she received news that the impending mar-riage had been abandoned mere weeks before the wedding was due to take place.

Sophia, empathetic and sympathetic, had ex-tended an invitation to Lily to visit indefinitely... an offer that had been graciously accepted.

Family held priority in life, Sophia insisted,

perhaps understandably more so, given Sophia and Giuseppe had been unable to have children of their own.

Alessandro slid out from behind the wheel, engaged the locking mechanism, then took a moment to breathe in the crisp late February evening air. A time of year that held the unpredictability of a lingering winter and the soft elusive hint of spring.

The dark night sky was heavy with the threat of rain, and he turned up the collar of his coat as he crossed towards the impressive well-lit front entrance with its double ornately carved wooden doors.

Doors that swung open within seconds of ringing the bell to reveal Carlo, Sophia's factotum, whose features held genuine pleasure.

'Alessandro. It is good to see you.'

'*Grazie*, Carlo.'

Both tall men in their late thirties, they went back a long way—years in fact—and shared a common history, to a degree. Sufficient enough to warrant a brief, but genuine male hand-clasp.

'Sophia?'

'Happy to have her god-daughter here.'

Words that conveyed much. For both men shared a silent bond to protect the one woman who had stood up to the plate for each of them. In their book, nothing, no one, could harm so much as a hair on her head without consequence.

Giuseppe had been a very successful businessman, whose villa bore discreet witness of his wealth. Beautifully patterned marble floors hosted an expansive foyer with exquisite furniture, a crystal chandelier whose prisms of sparkling light provided a spectacular setting for the double staircase curving to the upper floor.

A place Alessandro had been privileged to call *home* for the few years it had taken to conclude his schooling and later, during his university breaks. The sanctuary that, thanks to Giuseppe and Sophia, had offered him the opportunity to make something of his life.

'Alessandro.'

He turned at the sound of Sophia's voice, and he moved to greet her, settling his hands on her shoulders as he brushed his lips lightly to first one cheek, then the other before releasing her.

'You are well?' he queried gently, and received her smile in response.

'Of course, *caro*. It is good of you to join us.'

He lifted an eyebrow in musing query. 'You imagine I would refuse?'

Her answering smile brought one of his own. 'No.' She tucked an arm through his own. 'Come and meet the guests.'

Familiar faces of a select few, six in all, Alessandro perceived, as he acknowledged each and every one as Sophia drew him toward a slender petite young woman with sable hair styled in a classic knot, deep brown eyes and honey-gold skin.

Attractive, rather than classically beautiful, and possessed of a quality that set her apart. For there was a quiet strength apparent, a sense of self-preservation he recognized and admired.

'Lily.' Alessandro regarded her thoughtfully for a few seconds as he took her hand in his, glimpsed the unbidden flair of awareness evident as he leant forward to brush his lips to one cheek, then the other, and he caught the momentary tension before she swiftly recovered.

'Alessandro.' Her acknowledgment was accompanied by a polite smile as he released her hand.

In control, he perceived…and wondered idly

what it would take to break it. Only to immediately dismiss the thought. Lily was Sophia's niece...god-daughter, and *family*.

Yet something about her resonated with him, and he was inclined to discover why. The stirring of sensual chemistry together with the temptation to taste her generous mouth intrigued him.

'You are enjoying your stay with Sophia?' More than polite conversation, he mused, surprised to discover he was genuinely interested in her response.

A subtle perfume teased his senses...light, with a faint hint of warmth, woodsy, slightly floral with a tinge of musk, and something else he failed to define. Different from the more exotic fragrances favoured by many of his feminine companions. He wondered if she was aware it invited a closer examination, followed by the unbidden inclination to discover if the perfume was merely spritzed to various pulse-points, or applied as a lotion smoothed over her body.

'My aunt is very kind.'

'Sophia's generosity is well known.' Hence the instinctive protectiveness of those who had

Sophia's interests at heart. 'Your visit will give her much pleasure.'

Her mouth curved into a faint smile, and he found himself being fascinated by the slight dimple at the edge of her cheek.

'Please don't feel obligated to engage me in polite conversation,' she offered quietly.

His eyes sharpened a little. 'Is that what you think I'm doing?'

Her chin lifted fractionally. 'Isn't it?'

'No.'

'I wonder why I find it difficult to believe you.'

One eyebrow slanted as he regarded her thoughtfully. 'A lack of confidence in your personal charm?'

Oh, yes, that would do it. Except Lily refused to allow herself the indulgence.

Three days ago she'd arrived in Milan. A city where her late parents had been raised, educated, and had married before emigrating to Australia with their six-month-old daughter, Liliana—or Lily, as she was affectionately known—to begin a new life in Sydney.

An idyllic childhood, a good education—Lily

had excelled in every area of her life, qualifying as a chef and becoming a partner in her parents' restaurant. But then her parents' death three years ago in a car accident had left her suddenly in charge of the restaurant, an enviable inheritance, and one she had lived up to with the support of a few long-term friends.

A year ago she'd fallen in love, accepted James's ring, and had begun planning the big day. Only to return home early two weeks before their wedding to discover James in bed with a blonde, with whom, when pressed, he admitted he'd been conducting an affair for some months.

Lily had immediately thrown him out, despatched his clothes after him, returned his ring by courier, and promptly telephoned Sophia, her late mother's sister, to relay the wedding was cancelled. An invitation to visit had followed, and it had taken Lily only a few weeks to appoint a valued staff member to manage the restaurant, lease out the family home, store her car, and board a flight to Milan where she was duly met and driven to Sophia's beautiful Lake Como villa.

A delightful sanctuary, which offered tranquillity and the loving attention of a deeply caring aunt.

Three days in, Sophia had arranged a dinner for a few valued friends…a few of whom Lily remembered from a previous visit with her parents.

Including Alessandro del Marco.

It had been ten years since she'd last seen him in person…years that had shaped them both. For she was no longer a vulnerable young girl in her mid-teens, dazzled by the tall dark-haired young man whose almost black eyes held a dramatic mesh of blatant sensuality and elemental ruthlessness born from surviving on the streets for much of his youth.

There was a hardness apparent that reminded her of tempered steel, an edgy quality successfully masked beneath the cloak of sophistication—unyielding, almost primitive, and apparent to those who were sufficiently discerning to detect it.

As a young man in his mid-twenties, he'd fascinated her, stirring her imagination as she'd fantasized what it would feel like to have his mouth tutor her own. And more.

Had he known? *Hopefully not.*

A lot of water had passed beneath the bridge since then.

'Do you have any immediate plans?'

Lily rapidly collected her thoughts as she met Alessandro's dark gaze.

'Other than enjoying Sophia's hospitality?'

His faint smile held a glimmer of humour. 'Yes.'

She ruminated a little. 'I'd like to rent or lease a small apartment, and stay a while. Perhaps consider restaurant work.'

He studied her thoughtfully. 'You're serious about this?'

'Yes.' She had included her portfolio with just that thought in mind. A few months, more, even a year would provide a new perspective.

Change.

She'd ensured her financial assets in Australia were well protected. Who knew what life could hold?

Not marriage.

She was so over placing her trust in a man.

Alessandro indicated her empty glass. 'What are you drinking?'

Lily met his steady gaze, and shook her head. 'I'll wait and have wine with dinner.'

'A modest respect for alcohol, or a desire to be in control?'

She offered him a practised smile, and saw his eyes darken. 'Both.'

He wondered what it would take to have her relax her guard, to laugh a little with genuine amusement. And contemplated why it seemed important that she should.

Sophia wanted to assist in healing Lily's broken heart. For that reason alone, he would provide whatever Sophia considered necessary to ensure Lily's sojourn in Milan was as pleasant as possible.

Dinner comprised impeccably presented courses served with an appropriate wine. The intimate dinner setting contrived to seat Lily opposite Alessandro, ensuring that every time she lifted her gaze he was in her direct line of vision.

It was a distraction she didn't need, and during the main course she thought she caught his faint gleam of amusement...almost as if he knew his close proximity unsettled her.

Which it did. For there was something about

him that had the effect of heightening her senses and awakening an awareness she neither coveted nor wanted.

There, no matter how hard she attempted to ignore it.

'You will accompany Sophia next week.'

Lily gave her attention to the woman seated next to Alessandro. 'Thank you,' she managed with a polite smile. 'I'll look forward to it.' While silently wondering precisely *what* it was she had just agreed to look forward to.

'Fashion week,' Alessandro disclosed, almost as if he knew the passage of her thoughts. 'Sophia has managed excellent seating.'

It was easy to show genuine pleasure, and she did, for she adored fashion. 'How very kind of her.'

It was such a prestigious event, attended by fashionistas from all over the world. The crème de la crème of designers who engaged international models to display their labels, and there was much rivalry existent with behind-the-scenes drama…if one could believe reported gossip.

'You have your own restaurant, I believe?'

A courteous question to maintain conversation,

or merely politeness? Perhaps both, Lily allowed as she held the woman's attention.

'It originally belonged to my parents, and I spent time as a child in the kitchen, helping out, learning, and knew from an early age that I wanted to become a chef.'

Wonderful years, when knowledge of food, herbs and spices rolled off her tongue, and she could recite, unaided, the ingredients for most of the house specialties. How she loved to experiment, and reading recipe tomes became her pleasure.

'You studied overseas?'

'Initially Rome, then Paris.'

A time when life had helped fashion the young woman she had become. A connoisseur of food, and the skill to cook it to perfection. Equally fluent in French as she was in Italian as she boarded with families in both countries during her studies, learning from the professionals during class, while valuing age-old culinary tips and tricks from the women who shared recipes handed down from generation to generation. How a drop of this, a splash of that, the addition of a certain herb, could turn a simple sauce into an exquisite accompaniment.

A redolent aroma that begged a sample taste as it teased the nose with the promise of ambrosia.

'Yet you returned to Australia,' a fellow guest noted, and Lily returned her attention to the present.

'My family was there,' she relayed simply. 'Friends. It was where I wanted to be.'

And Parisi, the upmarket Italian-style restaurant her parents had worked so hard to achieve the stellar success it rightly deserved.

Hers now, with subtle additions to the menu, extra touches to the table settings, and slight changes to the decor.

There was pride in maintaining the high standard of quality food, excellent service, while ensuring a relaxed and happy atmosphere, where regular guests were welcomed by name with every effort made to secure their preferred table.

She'd imagined her life was mapped out…a brilliant business in a field for which she had a genuine love; a man she believed loved her; a wedding to plan.

Only for James to prove himself unfaithful, untrustworthy, and not the man she'd thought him to be.

There had been times over the past weeks when she'd shuddered at how close she'd come to committing to a marriage that held the portent of heartbreak and disaster.

A lucky escape, yet while it still hurt to think her trust had been betrayed, most of her anger was directed against herself for failing to recognize the *real* James beneath his practiced façade.

'And now you are here,' a light feminine voice concluded, bringing Lily back to the present. 'Sophia will adore having you join her on shopping excursions and ensure you enjoy the history that is Milan.'

'I'm looking forward to it.' She offered a smile that encompassed the guests seated opposite, and felt a start of surprise as she met Alessandro's steady gaze.

It was crazy, but she had the distinct feeling he'd discerned the passage of her thoughts and it rankled, stirring something deep inside she refused to acknowledge.

To be so conscious of him was unsettling, for it

made her feel uncomfortable, almost vulnerable, and she dismissed it, *him*, as she conversed with the guests.

Following the debacle with James, she wanted peace in her life, and a man of Alessandro del Marco's calibre was the antithesis of *calm*.

Sophia regarded Alessandro with immense affection, the son she and Giuseppe had made their own in all but name.

It was likely any invitation Alessandro extended to Sophia would include Lily while she remained a guest in Sophia's home.

So how difficult could it be?

The answer presented itself as the evening drew to a close, the guests departed, with Alessandro the last to leave.

'*Grazie*, Sophia,' he bade gently as he lowered his head and brushed his lips to each of her cheeks in turn before shifting to accord Lily a similar salutation.

Except in a bid for formality, she moved fractionally and to her utter embarrassment his lips touched her own…briefly, but it was enough to quicken her pulse.

Worse, she felt the insane desire to linger, to experience *more*...

For a moment her skin heated, and she took a hasty step backwards, misjudged the angle of her killer heels and clutched at his arm in an effort to maintain her balance.

Oh, hell. 'I'm sorry.' Had she said the words out loud? Hopefully not.

'My dear,' Sophia voiced with concern. 'Are you all right?'

'I'm fine,' Lily reassured, and knew it to be a lie.

Fine didn't cover it, when her pulse raced to a quickened beat, and sensation quivered deep within.

What was with that?

She didn't want to react emotionally to any man.

Especially not Alessandro del Marco.

Why, she didn't even *like* him.

Wrong, a silent voice accorded with impish intent. *You're afraid of how he might make you feel.*

Only a fool would travel that road.

Isn't going to happen, she assured with conviction.

Not in this lifetime.

So why this uncanny feeling *nothing* about her visit to Milan would follow any preconceived plan?

CHAPTER TWO

THE day Sophia had tickets for fashion week dawned cold, with drizzly rain, and Lily chose black leggings, soft leather calf-high black boots, an elegant knit thigh-length black dress, and added a long deep red cashmere scarf for contrast and extra warmth.

After a few days in Lake Como, she was still experiencing the transition from a southern Australian autumn to the close of a chilly northern Italian winter.

'Layers,' Sophia had advised. 'And pack an overnight bag with evening wear, for we will be attending one of the after-parties. Alessandro has insisted we stay overnight at his apartment to accommodate our shopping expedition tomorrow.'

Whoa. For a brief moment Lily vied between pleasure and mild apprehension.

The shopping expedition would prove delightful. But she had reservations about being a guest in Alessandro's apartment.

Reservations she determinedly dismissed on the grounds Sophia would be a fellow guest, and the only time they'd come face to face with their host would be breakfast…if then, for inevitably he'd leave early to begin the business day in his city office.

It was a matter of convenience, the combination of what would inevitably become a late night, and Alessandro was practically family.

So get over it.

Consequently an overnight bag became something more as she chose elegant red evening trousers and matching blouson top, black designer stilettos and a black evening bag. Together with sleep trousers, a cotton sleep vest, toiletries, make-up, and she was good to go.

In Carlo's capable hands the large Mercedes purred south from Sophia's Lake Como villa to Milan, entering the age-old city where traffic was intense, and it appeared every driver vied for position…often with a combination of high risk and dubious skill.

'Ah, we are almost there,' Sophia enthused as

the car slowed before turning into an entrance bay decked with carpet leading into the chosen venue.

Lily was unsure what to expect, but the sight of the paparazzi crowding in on each car as it arrived, the inevitable crush to determine *who* were the occupants, the brilliant flash bulbs popping, was incredible, and over the top.

'Your bags will be waiting for you at Alessandro's apartment,' Carlo relayed as Sophia and Lily exited the car.

'*Grazie*, Carlo,' Sophia offered in thanks. 'I'll be in touch with a time for our return.'

To say the day was an experience to remember didn't quite cut it, Lily mused as she became caught up with the sheer glamour, the personage of world-famous designers, the models and the Spring Collection fashions.

From avant-garde to almost bizarre, there were designs that were delightful, appealing and in a brilliant mesh of colours. Worn with professional panache by slender young models with sculptured hairstyles, perfect make-up, who held their heads high, eyes front, and rarely smiled.

Exquisitely aloof, Lily accorded, and couldn't

help wondering if there was pandemonium behind the scenes as egos clashed in discord.

Yet on the runway the presentation went like clockwork, there were envious nods from those in the audience who were contracted to record the day for numerous fashion magazines.

It was a privilege to be there, and Lily turned to Sophia as she offered a genuine thank you, accompanied by an impulsive fleeting kiss to her aunt's cheek.

'You are enjoying the day, *cara*?'

'Very much.'

There were some familiar personages present, women who held high positions with prestigious fashion magazines. New York, Paris, London. Easily recognizable were a few members of royalty, and three actresses seated front-row centre.

Then the music changed, and her attention returned to the runway where a famed designer provided an awe-inspiring cavalcade that drew murmurs of appreciation.

It was as the last in a series of models disappeared backstage that Lily experienced a faint prickle of awareness settle at the back of her neck, and she glanced at Sophia in time to see Alessandro slip into a seat next to her aunt.

There was a brief moment when she caught his smile, managed an acknowledging nod in response, and attempted to dispel his powerful image without much success.

He was an advocate of fashion?

Perhaps he was deciding to gift a designer original to his current mistress?

As if it were any concern of hers…

So why the sudden shaft of…*what?* Disappointment?

How crazy was that? She didn't even particularly *like* him. No, that wasn't entirely true. He aroused thoughts she didn't want to entertain with any man…especially *him*. So why this increased sense of awareness? Almost as if her body was at total variance with her mind.

Get with the programme, for heaven's sake, she silently bade as she focused her attention on the runway.

Sky-high heels, platform soles, boots—ankle, mid-calf and mid-thigh. Sandals with straps winding up to mid-calf. Fascinating, thrilling…

out of this world. And mostly impractical for everyday wear.

'I can almost feel my feet wincing in sympathy,' Sophia offered quietly, and Lily bit back a light chuckle.

'I suggest we leave soon,' Alessandro indicated. 'We'll have dinner, then return to my apartment to change in time to attend the after party at the hotel.'

'An excellent idea,' Sophia agreed, while Lily hid a degree of surprise.

Not to mention the faint onset of nerves. Crazy, she dismissed. Except she didn't want to experience the slight edginess his presence generated. Or the feeling he saw more than she felt comfortable with. For it was almost as if he could divine her mind…aware of the complexity of her thought process.

None of which sat well as she faced the evening in his company. Except what other choice did she have?

Alessandro chose an elegant restaurant full of *belle epoque* charm, which offered high quality fare Lily noted as she perused the menu.

Instead of a main, she selected an exquisite

pasta dish as an entree and opted for a light fruit confection for dessert.

Intimate table seating ensured she was aware of the subtle tones of his exclusive cologne, the clean smell of fresh linen…dammit, *him*…the masculinity he exuded with effortless ease, the sensual electricity apparent and a heightened sexuality that was intensely male.

Dangerous to her peace of mind, and other more intimate parts of her body.

How could she *feel* this way…*now*, when a matter of weeks ago she had been planning her own wedding to someone else?

It didn't make sense. Nor did it seem conceivable for the teenage crush she'd once had on Alessandro to linger in her subconscious mind for years, only to re-emerge with disturbing clarity when confronted with his presence.

Get over it, Lily bade silently.

Her own vulnerability, a combination of anger and hurt provided a *simple* explanation…one she chose to accept on the grounds that anything else defied analysis.

'Busy day, *caro*?' Sophia queried, and Lily

saw a warm smile curve Alessandro's generous mouth.

Doubtless wheeling and dealing multimillion-dollar takeovers formed part of his everyday life, Lily accorded silently.

'You were successful in acquiring the villa,' Sophia stated, and paused to take a sip of her wine before replacing the goblet on the table. 'It is charming, but in a sad state of disrepair.'

'But structurally sound,' Alessandro advised. 'I have a team of experienced craftsmen on standby to begin work as soon as the plans are approved.'

'A valuable investment,' Sophia concluded.

'An interest *and* a challenge,' Lily offered.

His dark eyes captured her own. 'Much like a woman,' he said smoothly, and glimpsed the momentary uncertainty before she quickly covered it with a degree of humour.

'Achieve the necessary work to reach your goal.' She paused imperceptibly. 'Then move on to the next challenge.'

'Inevitably with bricks and mortar,' he drawled, pinning her with his dark gaze. 'But not always with a woman.'

Why did she get the sudden impression she was

verging into dangerous waters? 'Yet you have not taken the plunge into marriage.'

'Are you concerned for my marital comfort?'

Oh, my. Erotic images momentarily filled her mind before she successfully dismissed them. 'Your progeny,' she managed evenly. 'And the future generation of Del Marco Industries.'

For a moment she thought she caught a wicked gleam in those dark eyes, then it was gone, and she put it down to her vivid imagination.

Sophia nodded. 'It is something of which I remind him on occasion.'

Why did the thought of Alessandro *married* cause her heart to plummet? And imagining him with another woman, a child or three...*hurt?*

It didn't make sense.

'Shall we order coffee?' Alessandro queried, and Sophia sent him a wry smile.

'Always you evade the issue.'

'And always I promise you will be the first to know when I find the right woman,' he said gently.

The sky was a dark indigo, and the air held an icy chill as they emerged from the restaurant a short while later.

It was a relief to reach Alessandro's car, the heating welcome as he took the north-west route to Magenta.

His apartment was situated on the P.za Sant Ambrogio, comprising two levels, and the height of luxury with marble-tiled floors, elegant oriental rugs, beautiful rosewood furniture in the lounge and reception rooms. Four guest bedroom suites were situated upstairs, including the master suite.

It wasn't the image Lily held of a bachelor pad. Somehow she'd expected something less... *refined.* Instead there was a quiet elegance apparent, *simpatico* with the building itself with its stucco exterior and ornate window framing illuminated by street lighting.

Whoever had organized the restoration had ensured the renovations combined modern-day luxury while maintaining the feel of a former era.

It was in a word...lovely. And Lily offered the compliment with sincerity.

'Grazie,' Alessandro inclined. 'It pleases me you approve. Will an hour be sufficient in which to shower and change?'

'With ease,' Sophia assured. 'Lily?'

'Of course.'

It took only minutes to unpack her overnight bag, discard her clothes and slip into the decadent marble en suite. For a moment she took an envious glance at the bath with its marbled surrounds and elegant fittings, before moving to the shower. A luxurious soak in decadent scented water was out of the question, and she quickly quelled the image as she turned the water dial.

There was no need to rush, and she took her time before drying off, then she wound a towel turban-style over her hair before slipping into fresh underwear, and tended to her make-up with a light hand, merely emphasizing her eyes, a touch of bronze blusher to each cheek, followed by a light gloss to her lips.

The classic little black dress with black stilettos was a safe choice.

She decided to sweep her hair into an elegant twist, which took several minutes to pin in place, and she added a subtle perfume to a few pulse points, attached diamond and ruby ear-studs and added a matching bracelet to her wrist.

Then she placed a red coat over her shoulders,

collected an evening purse and joined Sophia at the head of the stairs.

'You look lovely, *cara*,' Sophia complimented, and Lily smiled as she tucked a hand inside her aunt's elbow.

'So do you.' For Sophia bore a timeless elegance in whatever she chose to wear, she accorded with genuine admiration as they descended the stairs.

Alessandro was in the process of ending a call as they reached the spacious lounge, and she watched idly as he slipped the device into the inside pocket of his jacket before moving forward to greet them.

Attractive, intensely masculine in impeccable tailoring, white shirt in fine cotton, silk tie—he was something else, Lily perceived.

There was a depth to him, well hidden beneath the outer trappings his wealth could provide.

For a brief moment she sought to define it, and failed to adequately pin it down to any *one* quality.

Yet there was an instinctive sense of a need for self-preservation, a wariness that warned that when he played, he played to win. In any situation, be it a business deal, or a woman.

It wasn't difficult to imagine the type of woman he would seek. Tall, slender, beautiful, a socialite who would be the perfect hostess, please him in bed, bear him the requisite heir and turn a blind eye when he sought out a mistress.

'Charming,' Alessandro accorded with a smile that encompassed both women, and Lily caught the faint gleam of humour as his eyes caught and held her own.

For a brief moment she had the uncanny feeling he'd read her mind. Something she immediately dismissed as being ridiculous, for she wasn't that transparent…surely?

'Shall we leave?'

The hotel was situated adjacent the neighboring Botanical Gardens, and entrance into the hotel's exclusive lobby revealed beautiful fittings and furnishings.

Directions to a private lounge where the designer after party was being held were on display, and Security checked invitations at the door.

Once inside, Lily was met with a wave of the *beautiful* people, a few recognizable actresses, a model or three among them, and an abundance of glitz and glamour.

Members of the paparazzi were there with camera flashbulbs snapping the rich and famous, and the not too discreet journalists rapidly recording *names* as they matched *who* was with *whom*.

Voices filled the room, vying with background music which fought to be heard above snatches of Italian, French and English.

The people, the fashions, the sheer *ambience…* It was, in a word, *amazing*.

'Darling, you look absolutely stunning,' a light feminine voice offered in gushing tones. 'Who are you wearing?'

'A British designer who's making quite a name for herself.'

'Really. Who?'

The name was lost as another voice intruded, male, this time.

'Alessandro. Sophia.' Dark eyes settled on Lily. 'And this is?'

'Francesco,' Sophia acknowledged with polite charm. 'Allow me to introduce my niece, Lily. Francesco Alverro.'

A tall man, whose practiced smile appeared exactly that—practiced—as Lily took the hand he extended. And ignored the silent invitation in the intimate press of his thumb against her palm.

'We must get together.'

Not going to happen, she silently declined as she freed her hand.

'We have a number of social engagements planned over the next few weeks,' Sophia relayed with seeming regret.

'At a few of which we're bound to meet again.'

Lily felt the light touch of Alessandro's hand at her waist, and managed not to freeze into immobility. *What was he doing?*

'Perhaps,' Alessandro conceded smoothly. 'If you'll excuse us?'

Francesco inclined his head, eyes gleaming with wicked recognition for an instant before he stepped aside.

'I'm quite capable of judging men for myself,' Lily intoned quietly minutes later as a guest engaged Sophia in conversation.

'Of course you are,' he agreed with the barest hint of cynicism, and she wanted to *hit* him for alluding to her disastrous relationship with James.

'That was uncalled for.'

'You would do well to steer clear. Francesco

has a history of enjoying the chase, the capture, only to walk away.'

She met his dark gaze fearlessly. 'Don't most men?'

'Not always.'

'You, of course, are the exception,' she dismissed in droll tones. 'Which would explain why you've managed to avoid any commitment?'

His husky chuckle curled round her nerve-ends and tugged a little. 'Maybe I have yet to meet the one woman I would choose to share my life?'

'Someone sufficiently brave not to pander to your ego?'

'How…refreshing.'

'You think?' she offered with a faux smile, only to blink at a sudden flashbulb.

'A new conquest, Signor del Marco?' a feminine voice demanded, and thrust a small recording device close to him.

'A friend,' he responded with pseudo politeness, only to gain a knowing smile.

'Are you going to divulge the lady's name?'

Alessandro's silence earned a light laugh in response. 'I have my sources. Enjoy the party.'

'Interesting,' Lily declared with a tinge of

humour when the woman had moved out of ear-shot. 'Is it your celebrity or notoriety that draws attention?'

He subjected her to a steady appraisal. 'You possess a sassy mouth.'

A swift shaft of sensation arrowed deep within, and for a timeless second she felt the breath hitch in her throat, then she recovered.

'I believe it is a defence mechanism against men like you.'

'You have no knowledge of what manner of man I am.'

Believe me, I don't want to know.

So why this inclination to indulge in a tangle of words with him when instinct warned against it?

'Should I dare to offer a homespun psychological assessment?'

She caught a glimpse of wry humour in his dark eyes, then it was gone. 'You could try.'

Lily pretended to contemplate the challenge. 'I'll attempt a comparative balance,' she managed solemnly. 'In your favour, there is Sophia…for whom you would do almost anything. Even gifting time and support to her niece, which earns you several brownie points.' She held up a hand and figuratively ticked off one finger. 'I assume you're kind to young children and animals?' She barely paused as she counted off another finger. 'Of course you are. So let's move along. You're presentable, dress well, and possess a credible work ethic.' More than credible, but she chose not to linger.

'However, you have a certain—' Lily trailed deliberately. '—reputation. Which may be part fiction.' She pretended to contemplate the issue. 'Let's concede the jury is still out on that one.'

'Generous of you.'

She offered him a stunning smile. 'I'm glad you think so.'

There was a certain satisfaction to being in control, even temporarily. Yet she had the uncanny sensation it was *he* who held the strings.

Sophia rejoined them, and it was interesting to observe the guests shift singly and in small groups as the evening progressed.

In turn it was exciting to be part of it all, to simply observe the guests whose mission it was to be seen and impress; those who attended the various fashion weeks in other European capital cities and for whom designer after-parties were *de rigueur.*

Lily overheard voices raised in conflicting opinion over one particular designer's offerings on the runway.

'*Cara,* fashion is an art form, *presented* for visual appreciation of the designers' skilled technique with cloth and thread.'

'But, darling, who would consider wearing it?'

'A designer original speaks for itself.'

'And that is its attraction.'

'*Exactement.*'

Of course, Lily agreed silently as she scanned the room with interest, pausing when she sighted Sophia in deep conversation with a very attractive man.

Her aunt led a very full life with her involvement in a few select charities, together with an active social existence. She had once confided she'd chosen not to remarry, for her late husband had been her soulmate, and true love rarely struck twice.

For a moment Lily pondered the meaning of *soulmate*…two people so totally in tune with each other in every way, there could never be anyone else for either of them during their lifetime.

Had *she* felt that way about James?

In all honesty, she'd thought she *loved* him. Yet with the benefit of hindsight, she had to admit she'd loved the man she wanted him to be.

Rose-coloured glasses? Perhaps. From her perspective the relationship had felt right at the time. Although on reflection, she was able to pinpoint a few instances when she'd experienced slight niggles, little things she'd found mildly irksome, which she'd dismissed on the grounds she undoubtedly possessed a few irritating traits of her own.

Yet she'd enjoyed the sense they were a couple, with supposedly the same interests, and the sex, the intimacy had been…satisfactory.

James had wanted a short engagement, while she had been in no rush to legalize their relationship. It was James who had suggested they have a big wedding, and who had endeavoured to veto the small private ceremony she preferred.

He also had a liking for expensive clothes, the status symbols of wealth, but without the income to support them, given he regularly gifted financial assistance to his sister who resided in another state. Or so he had said.

Except the purported *sister* had turned out to be the lover she had faced sharing *her* bed in her own home.

Soulmate...to be so in tune with a partner, to know without doubt you were twin halves of a whole co-joined for life... Was it possible?

For some, perhaps.

'You're thinking too much.'

Alessandro's silky drawl lifted the fine hairs on her body, and there was no valid reason for the sudden spiral of sensation deep within.

Except it was *there*, like an ache that needed soothing...*ridiculous*.

Breathe, she bade silently as the tension between them became electric.

You're being fanciful, Lily silently chided. *Overly imaginative.* In the thrall of rampant hormones, the thought of which she found almost laughable.

Alessandro watched the play of fleeting emotions in her expressive eyes, and wondered if she realized how easily he could divine them.

On one level she fascinated him. For she possessed a conflicting mix of strength and vulnerability that made him feel…protective of her.

Even in killer heels the top of her head barely reached his shoulder, and he had an instinctive urge to remove the pins from her hair, knot its length with his fist and tug back her head to taste the sweet column of her throat, then savour the increased pulse-beat in the hollow at its base.

There was a bemused inclination to wonder how she'd feel in bed…*his*…her hair loose and tangled, her voice husky with passion as he drove her wild.

Not the most comfortable of contemplations, he perceived a trifle wryly as he caught a glimpse of Sophia on the point of rejoining them.

'I am so sorry,' Sophia apologized. 'I became caught up with one of the sponsors responsible for contributing to next week's charity gala.'

'Who undoubtedly agreed to increase his original donation,' Alessandro ventured, and was rewarded by Sophia's sparkling agreement.

'It is going to be a magnificent event. Tomorrow,' she added, gifting Lily a warm smile, 'we shop for something spectacular for each of us to wear.'

'Sounds like a plan,' Lily agreed.

It was late when Sophia suggested they should leave, and Lily glanced idly at the well-lit streets as Alessandro negotiated traffic.

The after-party had been a fascinating experience, completing an exceptional day…and Lily said as much as they entered Alessandro's apartment.

'Thank you,' she added with genuine appreciation, and gave Sophia a warm hug. Then she turned towards Alessandro and offered a smile. *'Grazie.'*

'My pleasure.'

His dark gaze encompassed them both. 'Shall we have coffee?'

'I'll pass,' Lily declined, 'and head for bed.'

'Sleep well, *cara*,' Sophia bade gently, and watched Lily ascend the stairs, aware Alessandro's attention mirrored her own. With a quiet smile she tucked a hand beneath his arm. 'Let's have that coffee.'

In the kitchen he spooned ground coffee beans into the espresso machine, then he filled two demitasse cups with the dark aromatic brew, set both cups on the table and gave the woman seated opposite a quizzical look.

'This is not about the coffee.'

Sophia met his gaze with a degree of solemnity. 'No.'

He took a seat and offered a wry smile. 'Lily.'

Sophia was silent for a few measurable seconds. 'I would hate to see her hurt,' she said gently.

'Will it ease your mind if I assure you that is not my intention?'

'*Sì.*'

A simple affirmative, one she had no hesitation in giving. '*Buona fortuna*, Alessandro.'

Dark eyes gleamed with a tinge of humour. 'I may need it.'

CHAPTER THREE

IT TOOK ages for Lily to fall asleep, for however much she tried she couldn't dispel Alessandro's powerful image, or justify the disturbing awareness that arose whenever she was in his presence.

He seemed imprinted in her mind…*there,* a vivid haunting constant that heightened her senses, teasing how his mouth would feel on her own, the touch of his hands…

Stop right there!

Such thoughts hardly made sense, and she did her best to dispense with them, attempting to qualify the fact she slept in a guest suite on the same floor as *his* suite as being responsible for her heightened awareness.

Anything else was madness.

Tiredness eventually won out, and she woke feeling ready to face the day.

Showered and dressed, she moved downstairs

and discovered her aunt seated in the dining room sipping coffee.

'Good morning, *cara*,' Sophia greeted with a smile. 'You slept well?'

'Yes, thanks…and you?'

Sophia inclined her head and indicated the chair opposite. 'Join me for breakfast. Alessandro left early for the office.'

The faint knot in her stomach relaxed a little, for the thought of facing him across the breakfast table hadn't sat well.

The tempting aroma of coffee permeated the air, and there was a carafe of orange juice, together with a few cloche-covered dishes resting on the table.

It was a perfect way to begin the day.

'Carlo will collect us in half an hour and be at our disposal before we head back to Lake Como,' Sophia relayed, and Lily offered an impish grin.

'Sounds like fun.'

Her aunt laughed. 'It will be. Serious shopping is on the agenda.'

No idle promise, Lily perceived as Sophia focused their attention on the *quadrilatero* situated in the heart of Milan.

'We will begin with Via Montenapoleone,' Sophia stated knowledgeably, sparing Carlo a twinkling smile. 'Familiar territory, is it not?'

'Indeed. I have extensive knowledge of every shop.'

'Carlo is very patient,' her aunt confided with a light laugh. 'He is my driver, he accompanies me on shopping excursions, and he also acts as bodyguard.'

Bodyguard?

'Merely a protective measure,' Carlo informed.

The question had to be *why* it was deemed necessary.

'Do not look so concerned,' Sophia bade gently. 'Since Giuseppe's death, Alessandro and Carlo have taken it upon themselves to escort me wherever I choose to go.'

Two strong masculine men, each a recipient of Giuseppe and Sophia's benevolence during their youth, who cared enough to give of their time, their resources, to ensure Sophia's safety and well-being.

It was a commendable act, and one Lily could only admire.

'Let's begin, shall we?'

She gave her aunt an infectious smile. 'Lead the way.'

It came as no surprise when Sophia was greeted by name and afforded deferential treatment at many of the shops they visited.

'The Charity Gala, *signora?* For you?'

'And my niece, Lily.'

'Ah, I have the perfect gown. So elegant.' She paused as she considered Lily's slender curves and height. 'For Lily, perhaps something from the Spring Collection. An opaque floral silk chiffon in delicate shades of powder blue, lavender, with a hint of pink. There is simplicity in the style, and with your hair swept high…' Her head tilted a little. 'Or the red, *sì*, the red would be stunning with your colouring. We shall view them both.'

Of the two, Lily adored the red silk chiffon with its bias cut skirt, ruched bodice. Elegant, the design showcased her delicate shoulders, narrow waist, and Sophia clapped her hands together as she accorded it *perfectto.*

'We will take both.' Her eyes twinkled with pleasure and she lifted a hand at Lily's protest. 'It is my gift to you.' A light laugh escaped her as she took hold of Lily's hand and lifted it to her lips. 'All these years I am your godmother, and there have been so few opportunities for us to spend time together.'

'*Zia*, please. It is much too generous.' She turned towards the vendeuse. 'The red gown, for which I shall pay.'

'*Cara*, we will not argue.'

'We have exquisite stilettos to match the gown.' As if by magic the delicate shoes were presented for approval, and as promised, they were perfect.

'Lily, you may pay for the stilettos,' Sophia conceded graciously. 'But that is all I will allow.'

It was an exceedingly beautiful gift and a very special memory she would treasure for a very long time, and she said so as she hugged her aunt with genuine appreciation.

'Now I shall stand strong,' Lily insisted as they emerged onto the street. 'Lunch is on me, at a restaurant of your choice.' She paused fractionally, then lobbied with an impish twinkle, 'We will not argue, *sì*?'

Sophia gave a delighted laugh. 'You remind me so much of your mother, when, as single young women, we shopped together.'

Carlo retrieved their signature-emblazoned

carry-bags, and spared both women a musing look. 'Success?'

'Indeed,' Sophia agreed. 'Yet we are far from done.'

Carlo merely smiled. 'Of course not.'

Together they strolled towards Via Manzoni, pausing frequently to browse the shops, venturing into a few, purchasing items that enchanted the eye, as Sophia and Carlo pointed out places of historic interest, the aristocratic *palazzi* along Via Manzoni, the Grand Hotel, the Archi di Porta Nuova, a city gate once part of the medieval walls.

There was a sense of timelessness, a lingering knowledge of centuries past, and how life must have been then in comparison to today's era.

Lunch offered a leisurely respite, and they sampled excellent cuisine, shared a light white wine, concluding with coffee before they emerged onto the street to visit a famed *museo* where paintings graced the walls and precious ceramics were featured.

It was Sophia who suggested they dine before returning to Lake Como, and Carlo drove them to a charming little *osteria* owned by a couple who made divine pasta sauce. So much so, Lily savoured the taste with a view to determining an elusive ingredient.

'I have tried to persuade the chef to divulge the secret of his sauce,' Sophia confided. 'All he will do is smile, lift his hands and offer "a bit of this, a touch of that". Incredible, is it not?'

'A hint of chilli, unless I'm mistaken,' Lily posed in contemplation. 'With perhaps a sprinkle of brown sugar to sweeten. And scallions, I think, for their crisp light taste.'

'You would like to experiment in my kitchen?'

Lily offered an impish smile. 'Perhaps we can experiment together. Tomorrow?'

'I'd like nothing better.'

'Such an honour,' Carlo declared. 'Only Alessandro has been permitted to try his hand in Sophia's kitchen.'

Lily raised an eyebrow. 'Alessandro?'

'He worked kitchens in places no respectable person knew existed,' Sophia revealed, sobering a little. 'Liaised deals with undesirables likely to double-deal or worse, rather than pay up. And sleep anywhere he could find a place to lay his head.'

'Always on the alert, and with means of protection,' Carlo added quietly.

Lily looked at him carefully. 'You speak from experience.' It wasn't a question, merely a statement.

'Yes.'

'As one of Alessandro's…partners.' She refrained from adding…*in crime*.

'An interesting description,' Carlo conceded in a lightly accented drawl.

An understatement, if ever there was one, Lily conceded, aware the reality had been far worse than either man would admit.

It was late when Carlo brought the car to a halt outside the main entrance to Sophia's villa, and he delivered their purchases indoors, refused coffee, and bade both women *buona notte*.

Lily turned to Sophia as Carlo left, and issued genuine thanks for a wonderful day.

'You're most welcome, *cara*.' Sophia hugged Lily close. 'We will sort our purchases in the morning. Goodnight, Lily,' she bade gently. 'Sleep well.'

'You, too, *Zia*.'

Together they ascended the staircase, then parted as Lily moved to her guest suite.

The large bed looked inviting, and she removed her clothes, took a leisurely shower, then she slid between the sheets and fell asleep almost as soon as her head hit the pillow.

It was almost seven when she woke, and she stretched her limbs, then she threw back the covers and padded to the set of windows, tilted the indoor shutters and watched in admiration as sunrise coloured the gardens to a beautiful kaleidoscope of landscaped glory.

A new day lay ahead, and she completed her morning routine before choosing dress jeans and a casual top, then she slid her feet into flat shoes and was about to leave the room when she remembered to check her laptop.

There were several emails awaiting her attention, a few of which she quickly skimmed before reaching an update from Parisi's manager reporting that all was going well in the restaurant.

The sender of the next email was *James,* and her initial reaction was to delete it unread. Except curiosity led her to the deleted folder minutes later, and she read the apologetic missive, citing

his remorse, heartbreak, and the plea for reconciliation, followed by a promise to be loyal and
loving…if only she'd give him another chance.

It didn't even qualify an answer.

Without pause she closed the laptop and made
her way downstairs to find Sophia sipping coffee
at the dining-room table while she perused the
daily newspaper.

'Good morning, *cara*,' Sophia greeted with a
warm smile, and indicated the table's contents.
'Coffee? Juice?'

Lily slid into a chair and helped herself to juice,
drank it slowly.

'Some of the fashions from the runway are
written up.' Sophia indicated the page in question. 'Together with photos from the party. This
week's trade magazines will feature both in more
detail.' She moved the newspaper so Lily could
view it.

Lily had no problem reading the Italian script,
and she skimmed over the photographs, then
came to a halt as she recognized one of her standing next to Alessandro at the party.

Except it wasn't so much the photo that drew
her attention, but the teasing caption speculating

her identity, and if *she* was his latest romantic interest. Concluding with *watch this space*.

It angered her that innuendo and supposition combined with clever angle photography lent evidence to there being a grain of truth to the gossip.

'Where do they get this stuff?' Lily demanded over a second cup of coffee.

'*Cara*, don't allow it to distress you,' Sophia attempted to soothe. 'It's how the media makes a living, and Alessandro has a propensity to attract attention.'

'Which I don't choose to share.'

Sophia commiserated in silence, all too aware Lily had captured Alessandro's interest. She knew him so well, better than most...enough to recognize the occasions when he merely played the social game. Somehow she very much doubted this was one of them.

'Have something to eat, then we shall attempt to duplicate pasta sauce, hmn?'

As a distraction ploy, it worked, as they combined experience, instinct and flair to create what promised to be ambrosia.

'What do you think?' Sophia queried as she

dipped a spoon into the simmering sauce and held it out for Lily to taste.

'Close.' So very close, but something was missing. She made a sudden decision. 'Another pinch of brown sugar, and I'm going to add a bay leaf. Maybe that'll do it.'

'This is so much fun. I remember *Mamma* would make her own pasta and teach your mother and me how to make *panini*. Her kitchen was always the focal point of our house, filled with different aromas. She had the most comprehensive herb garden…and her vegetables were the best tended in the village.'

'I've heard some of the stories…how the chickens each had names,' Lily declared with a warm laugh.

'There were a few ducks, turkeys, and a pig you named Mirabella.'

Sophia chuckled. 'Poor Mirabella. She didn't realize she was a pig. I woke one morning and she wasn't there.' She shook her head. '*Papa* explained, *Mamma* consoled…but I haven't been able to eat pork since.'

While the sauce continued to simmer they took

out fine flour, eggs and made pasta, which they ate for lunch with fresh crusty bread.

'Hmm, this is so good,' Sophia complimented, while Lily lifted a hand and tilted it back and forth.

'But not quite *right*.' Her forehead creased a little. 'Next time I'll ditch the bay leaf and add a pinch of paprika.'

'Lily, this dish would draw genuine praise in the finest restaurant.' Sophia's eyes lit with a mischievous sparkle. 'You are bent on a mission.'

'Uh-huh.'

'But not today,' her aunt said firmly. 'This afternoon Alessandro is taking you on a scenic tour of the lakes. There is much to see.'

Alessandro? 'I'm sure he's much too busy,' Lily protested, only to see Sophia shake her head.

'If that were so, he would not have offered.'

The fact that he had disturbed her more than she was prepared to admit. *Why* seemed a logical query, for which she had no sensible answer.

Lily was ready at the appointed time, attired in tailored black trousers, a fine red cashmere sweater beneath a tailored black jacket, with comfortable black flats on her feet.

Alessandro's sleek black car slid to a halt adjacent the entrance, and it appeared he'd chosen comfort over formality, given the absence of a tie, the few top buttons of his shirt open, to which he'd added a butter-soft leather black jacket.

It gave him a rakish look, one he wore with remarkable ease, she perceived as he greeted Sophia before turning towards Lily.

'Shall we leave?'

Sophia was right, Lily determined as Alessandro drove into the hills to a vantage point where the splendid vista of lakes stretched north to the snow-capped mountains in the distance.

Below there were clutches of villages nestling close to the lakes; villas with terracotta roof tiles providing colour among the tree-clad hills, the calm blue-grey waters where a few speedboats towed water-skiers and two jetskis left plumes of white spray behind them.

'Como produces a large percentage of Europe's silk,' Alessandro revealed. 'We will visit the Museo della Seta, and La Tessitura, a store owned by a leading designer of luxury silk.' He gestured to the panoramic scenery. 'There is so much history here.'

'Relative serenity, should one choose it,' Lily conceded. 'And the advantage of its proximity to Milan.'

Italy was the country of her birth and she had a strong inclination to stay a while. There was an instinctive desire to rediscover her roots, to enjoy the land, its people. Whatever life chose to offer…

She stifled a reflective sigh. She could live here, enjoy the ambience…the lifestyle, the food, Sophia… It was tempting, and she had nothing to lose.

There were so many places of interest, the stunning villas and their history.

'Were you born in Milan?' The query emerged from her lips without thought, and she bore his brief glance before he returned his attention to the road.

'According to my birth certificate.'

'Your parents moved around a lot?'

'It depends on your interpretation of the word.'

Lily was silent for several seconds. 'That bad?'

And then some. Memories, images that would remain with him for the rest of his time on this earth.

'I managed to survive.'

She looked at him carefully. 'But not easily.'

Not on the right side of the law...until Giuseppe dalla Silvestri had provided an opportunity for a new life.

'I was fortunate to be born into a loving family,' she offered quietly when he didn't answer. 'Caring parents who gifted me a great childhood, insisting I had a good education and the advantage of extending my studies overseas. My life,' she added. 'Encapsulated in two sentences.'

'You left out the ex-fiancé.'

'Intentionally.'

'A closed subject?'

'For now.' She shot him a perceptive glance. 'As I imagine you regard details of your youth.'

A wry smile curved his generous mouth.

A man who guarded his privacy, she perceived, and couldn't fault him for it. She wasn't exactly comfortable relaying every little detail about her broken engagement.

It took time and a vast degree of trust to bare one's soul.

Maybe one day... *Where did that come from?*

Alessandro wouldn't become part of her life, any more than she would form part of his own.

He was merely being kind to Sophia's niece... yet there was the unbidden thought that Carlo could easily have acted as guide and companion.

'I hope taking time from the office isn't intruding on your workload.'

Alessandro eased the powerful car to a halt at a vantage point and closed the engine.

The view, magnificent as it was, only briefly held her attention as he shifted in his seat to face her, and suddenly the space inside the car seemed too confined. For his attention was no longer focused on negotiating the snakelike roads winding through the hills.

'Concern for my business interests, Lily?'

There was a teasing quality to his slightly accented voice that curled round her nerve-ends and heightened her awareness of him. The fine lines fanning out from the outer corners of his eyes; the faint groove slashing each cheek; his generous mouth, which momentarily trapped her gaze.

What was with the sudden temptation to lightly explore it? Trace its curve with her fingers...

more, reach forward and touch his lips with her own. Almost as if some inner force was in play.

It hardly made sense, yet it was there, a hidden magnetic quality she fought hard to dismiss.

'I'm sure you possess a coterie of highly qualified staff eminently capable of handling whatever needs to be handled,' she managed lightly. 'As well as the latest device in communication technology to enable instant contact if need be.'

His expression was impossible to determine, and her eyes widened as he trailed light fingers along the edge of her jaw, cupped it and pressed a thumb to her lower lip.

Did hearts stop? It felt as if her own did. Certainly she consciously ceased breathing for several timeless seconds, locked in mesmerized fascination as he leant in close and brushed his lips to her temple.

His scent teased her senses, stirring them alive, and her mouth parted a little on a soundless sigh.

It would be so easy to frame his face and seek his mouth with her own…to taste and savour, *discover* the magic of his touch.

Yet something held her back. Uncertainty? A

need to retain the emotional defences she'd acquired since James's traitorous behaviour?

So why did she feel slightly bereft when Alessandro released her and undid his seat belt?

'The sunset is spectacular from here.' He slid out from behind the wheel and strode round the car to open her door.

'Let's watch it together, then we'll find somewhere to eat.'

'I think Sophia is expecting me for dinner.' It was a token protest which resulted in his faint smile.

'Not when I assured her I'd return you to the villa by eleven.'

Her lips parted in surprise. 'I don't...'

'A meal, Lily, with pleasant conversation?'

It sounded innocuous. After all, what did she have to fear?

'You neglected to include the sunset.' With that she slid from the passenger seat and walked the guard-rail, aware that he stood at her side.

The colours gradually changed and deepened as the sun sank beyond the horizon, flaring in one last burst as dusk settled and the evening sky darkened.

'If we wait, you'll see the stars emerge,' Alessandro informed quietly as he moved to stand behind her.

His close proximity stirred her already awakened senses, and she stilled as he wrapped an arm about her waist and leant in close.

She should step aside, put some distance between them, and she almost did. Except his arm, his presence, made her feel...protected. Safe, she added silently, declining to examine precisely why.

'Watch closely,' Alessandro bade, directing her attention.

And there they were, tiny pinpricks of light in the sky, gradually appearing brighter as the night's darkness assumed a deep indigo. A beautiful backdrop for the illumination of villas and street-lighting of towns spread out below them.

He was tempted to seek the soft hollow at the edge of her nape. To shift his hands to her midriff and let them slide up to cup her breasts. To pull her in close and allow her to feel the strength of his arousal.

Knowing if he made even one of those moves,

any pleasure he gained would be exceedingly temporary. And he didn't want *temporary*.

'Food, I think,' he suggested lightly as he stepped back. 'There's a trattoria a few kilometres from here. Their fare is family oriented and good.'

He was right, Lily concluded as she ordered lasagne, a side salad and fresh bread with olive oil and herbs for dipping.

There was music, the soft lilt of a guitar and piano accordion accompanying a handsome young man as he sang the traditional songs of his homeland.

This was the Italy she loved. Good food, a little wine, fine music and the company of a pleasant companion.

A very attractive man, with rugged features, dark piercing eyes that saw more than she felt comfortable with, and whose attention she was at a loss to define.

'You are enjoying yourself.'

Her eyes held a pleasurable sparkle as she gifted Alessandro a warm smile.

She had eaten every morsel of her lasagne, finished the salad, declined dessert, and chosen tea instead of coffee.

A woman who ate with a genuine appetite, instead of the token salad sans dressing together with a minuscule serving of fresh fruit that passed as an evening meal, made for a pleasant change, Alessandro mused as he sipped his coffee.

'It's been a lovely day.' It was the truth, she acknowledged simply. 'Thank you.'

He took hold of her hand and lifted it to his lips. 'My privilege.'

Her eyes widened a little as she met his own, and for a few timeless seconds she couldn't look away.

I don't know where you're going with this. Worse, why did she have this instinctive feeling he was several steps ahead of her? Steps leading *where*? Surely nowhere other than friendship.

And if so, why the sense of disappointment? It didn't make sense.

Because you don't want it to make sense.

Such contrariness didn't bode well for her peace of mind as she gathered her composure. 'Shall we leave?'

Alessandro summoned the waitress, paid the bill, then he rose to his feet and escorted Lily from the trattoria.

It was almost eleven when they drew to a halt outside the entrance to Sophia's villa, and she released her seat belt with one hand and reached for the door-clasp with the other.

'I have my key,' Lily said quickly. 'There's no need for you to...'

Except he had already slid out from the car, and her remaining words remained unsaid as he crossed to her side, took the key from her fingers and inserted it into the front door.

'Goodnight, Lily,' he intoned gently. 'I'll see you tomorrow evening.'

She looked at him blankly.

'A party given by one of Sophia's dearest friends to celebrate her daughter Anabella's engagement,' Alessandro revealed.

How could it have slipped her mind? 'Of course. Sophia mentioned it this morning. Goodnight.' She moved indoors, locked up and reset the alarm as Sophia had demonstrated, then she crossed the foyer and ascended the stairs to her suite.

* * *

A small dinner party with friends to celebrate the host's daughter's engagement would make for a pleasant evening, Lily reflected as she ran a last-minute check. Black evening trousers, a stunning red silk chiffon blouse, black cropped jacket, which she'd remove on arrival, evening purse, black stilettos. Hair in an elegant upswept knot, diamond ear-studs, pendant and bracelet.

Good to go, she decided as she exited her suite and descended the stairs to join Sophia in the lobby.

'Have I kept you waiting?'

'Not at all,' Sophia reassured. 'Alessandro has just arrived. I was about to open the door.'

Which she did, and he stood in the wide aperture, a tall dark-haired figure in an immaculately tailored suit, exuding an overwhelming sense of masculine power.

'Sophia, Lily.'

'Caro,' Sophia greeted with a smile as she accepted the brush of his lips to her cheek, while Lily flashed him a silent *please don't* message, which he naturally ignored.

This close, even briefly, he stirred her senses and sent the blood coursing through her veins as she took in the subtle aroma of his cologne, the faint hint of freshly laundered clothing.

For one totally wild moment she had the craziest feeling her body swayed towards his of its own accord, something she immediately corrected, and missed the faint narrowing of his eyes.

Everything took on a different look at night, Lily mused as the car took a route leading towards the hills. Lights sparkled in the distance, providing a delicate tracery against the indigo sky.

Small was a misnomer, Lily decided as she saw the number of cars lining a large circular driveway leading to a magnificent three-storied villa set in beautiful softly illuminated grounds.

They were greeted by their host, then escorted by a staff member to what could only be termed a large ballroom where an impressive number of guests mingled while staff circled offering trays of canapés, champagne and wine.

Lily recognized a few familiar faces, guests she'd met on a few previous occasions over the past week, and during the ensuing half hour she received introductions to those remaining.

As well as the host's daughter, Anabella, and her fiancé Enrico.

The couple looked so happy, with eyes only for each other, and the secret smile that lovers had, convinced that *love* alone would surmount whatever life could throw at them.

Had *she* been that happy on the night of her engagement to James? *Content* was the word that came to mind. Aware, perhaps, that she had everything she needed, having achieved much, and settling with a good partner was the next step.

At the time she'd thought it was love. How *wrong* she had been.

Focus, Lily bade silently. *You discovered the fallacy and escaped before any real damage was done. Not all men are like James.* Yet her confidence in judging men had taken a battering. It was simpler to avoid them, and as for considering a relationship…forget it.

A light touch at her waist brought her sharply back to the present as Alessandro settled his hand at the small of her back, and a slight feathery sensation slid down her spine.

Nerves, she accorded…and knew it was more.

Awareness. Sensual recognition. Sexual chemistry.

All three. And nothing she did, even attempting psychological analysis, and how crazy was that, was successful in diffusing the warmth, the heat, he generated in her body.

Not once in her life had she experienced such a reaction or felt so confused by it.

Hopefully any minute soon Alessandro would choose to mix and mingle, acknowledge friends and she could breathe easily again.

Except he remained at her side...*there,* almost as if he knew his presence affected her, and determined to press the advantage.

'Sophia, a moment of your time, if you please.'

'Of course,' her aunt granted graciously as she excused herself and moved away a few paces to confer.

'Nothing to say, Lily?' Alessandro posed lightly, and she found it remarkably easy to summon a stunning smile.

'What would you like to discuss? Fiscal affairs, the current oil spill? That should fill a void.'

He lifted a hand and trailed light fingers down her cheek, caught a glimpse of fleeting emotion in her eyes before it was quickly masked. Pain? Vulnerability? Perhaps *both*…and wondered why it should matter so much. 'You have no need to feel nervous,' Alessandro said gently.

She didn't want *gentle*. *Dammit*, she didn't want to play the musing conversational game—light innocuous words without substance that meant little.

'Why should I be nervous?' For a moment she held his gaze, and his soft laughter curled round her nerve-ends. Not the most comfortable sensation, Lily admitted as she held up a hand and began ticking off each finger.

'Today I've had breakfast with Sophia, a sojourn in Como, shopping, followed by lunch, and more shopping.'

'That is all?'

No, it wasn't. Except she had no intention of revealing another email from James had appeared in her inbox, a further missive citing remorse, empty promises and begging for another chance. Another email she'd chosen to ignore.

She tilted her head a little and regarded him with deliberate solemnity. 'Why don't you tell me about *your* day?'

Alessandro's eyes gleamed with humour. 'Corporate meetings, a linked video conference, lunch with an associate.'

'And now you're here, socializing and doing duty with Sophia's niece.'

'Is that how you perceive my presence?'

'It's not?'

'No.'

For a few brief seconds she became lost for words, unable to summon *any* that made sense, and the sassy response that rose to her lips remained unsaid.

At that moment their host announced dinner was due to be served, and requested the guests be seated.

Name cards designated placings, and Lily felt her stomach execute a slow somersault as she realized she was seated at Alessandro's right, with Sophia to his left.

The arrangement would offer no respite from his presence for an hour, *two* hours, she eventually amended, and they were yet to raise a toast to the newly engaged couple.

Alessandro proved to be an attentive male companion, maybe a little too attentive as he appeared to regard her with a degree of affection, ensuring her glass was filled, solicitously abiding by her request for mineral water after the initial flute of champagne. *There,* adding supposition to innuendo that she was *more* than merely Sophia's niece. The light brush of his hand, the warm smile.

Charm, he possessed it in spades. Although only a fool would fail to detect the ruthless edge beneath his sophisticated persona.

It was a combination that appeared to fascinate, Lily perceived, as she noted covert glances from, not one, but three attractive women seated at the table…not that she was counting, of course.

A subtle invitation in the soft parting of perfectly glossed lips and a slow delicate sweep of the tongue.

Was it his expertise between the sheets that attracted these women or the fortune he'd managed to amass?

Inevitably *both,* she decided with unaccustomed cynicism.

Hadn't it been James's modus operandi to act a part, then offer he needed a *real* woman prepared to meet *all* his sexual needs as his excuse for maintaining an affair?

'*Attenzione.*'

This was the moment to fill flutes with champagne and toast the newly engaged couple, something which was achieved with voiced enthusiasm.

Lily banked down the faint stirring of envy as she took in the radiant Anabella and the equally enamoured Enrico.

Had *she* been so enchanting, and glowing with love on the evening she'd accepted James's ring?

There had been pleasure, certainly, and contentment...but *glowing?*

Not really. And there was the thing: what had felt sensible at the time, hadn't been *right* from the beginning.

A slight shiver slid down her spine as Alessandro stretched a casual arm across the back of her chair and leaned towards her to quietly offer, 'Beautiful, is she not?'

This close she was aware of the warmth from his body, the intense masculinity he projected with effortless ease.

'Stunning,' Lily conceded as she met his gaze

with what she hoped was polite indifference, and felt betrayed by an increased beat of the pulse at the base of her throat.

It was a relief when dinner concluded and their hosts encouraged guests to move into the adjoining ballroom where a DJ began to play so the guests could dance.

Mood music alternated with upbeat modern, and Lily deliberately sought to mingle a little, aware Alessandro rarely moved from her side.

'Dance with me.'

Lily felt her eyes widen momentarily before she successfully masked her expression. A silent *no* rose and died in her throat at the thought of being enclosed in his arms moving to slow music beneath dimmed lighting.

'I think…'

'Don't,' he said quietly, and drew her onto the dance floor and into his arms.

Relax. She could do this. They were in the middle of a dance floor in a large room filled with people.

So why did she feel as if…*what?*

As if they were the only two people in the room and no one else existed.

It shouldn't feel this good. To be perfectly in tune with every move, almost as if they'd danced together in a previous life. Madness, she mentally discounted.

His hold was loose, almost formal, yet instinct warned he would draw her close in against him if she attempted to put any distance between them.

Almost as if he sensed the pattern of her thoughts he pulled her in, and *formal* went out of the window.

Oh, my.

The breath hitched in her throat as he slid a hand down her spine to settle at its base.

This close his cologne teased her senses, meshing with freshly laundered clothing and the faint muskiness of man.

A sensual magic that swirled round her senses and stirred a longing for the impossible. It was easy to blame the haunting music and lyrics; the man who held her.

Perhaps something too complex to fully comprehend.

All she knew was the desire to capture the moment and hold onto it for as long as she could.

Inevitably the slow track concluded, the beat

changed and Lily excused herself on the pretext of offering her congratulations to the newly engaged couple, before seeking to compliment the hostess on a lovely evening, and offer her thanks for the invitation.

'You are most welcome. Sophia is a very dear friend, and it is a delight to have you join her tonight. I trust you are enjoying your visit here?'

'Very much, thank you.'

Coffee, hot, strong and black with sugar, Lily decided as she made her way towards a table set to one side where staff were dispensing espresso. She accepted a cup, sipped the contents and had almost finished when she heard her name.

'Lily.'

There was only one male voice whose slightly accented voice caused her pulse to accelerate, and she turned towards him.

'Alessandro,' she acknowledged with a smile. 'Seeking coffee, too?'

'You.'

Well, that's succinct. 'Really?' She indulged in a deliberate pause. 'Is there a particular reason?'

'Several.' He let that statement stand alone. 'For the moment, *one* will suffice.'

'And that is?'

She was something else, Alessandro acknowledged with wry humour as he curved an arm across the back of her waist.

'Sophia is ready to leave.'

Lily attempted to put some distance between them, without success, as they stood together in the foyer while Sophia chatted with their hosts before moving out to the car.

Lily focused her attention on the faint tracery of lights as Alessandro's car descended the winding road. It was late, and Alessandro's attention during the evening filled her mind as she attempted to make sense of it.

Yet he fascinates you, an inner voice prompted.

So what if he does?

Maybe you should discover why.

Not any time soon, she assured silently. She'd already suffered one betrayal, why would she discard sanity and risk another?

It was a relief to reach the gates guarding her aunt's spacious villa, and once indoors Alessandro bade them goodnight and leaned in to brush his lips to Sophia's cheek before choosing Lily's mouth in a light evocative caress that was over before it had really begun.

As he intended.

He caught the faint flare of helpless emotion in her eyes, then it was gone as she crossed the foyer and ascended the stairs to her suite.

It didn't help knowing he occupied a guest suite not far from her own or that her imagination went into overdrive as she mentally pictured him discarding his clothes, one by one until nothing covered his impressive muscular frame.

And that was where mental imagery had to cease...

CHAPTER FOUR

IT WAS something of a relief to discover Alessandro had already left when Lily joined Sophia for breakfast the following morning.

'He is attending a conference in Paris today, another in London tomorrow,' Sophia declared. 'Which gives me the opportunity to show you a few of the most famed historic places in Milan— art galleries, a wonderful palazzo, the Duomo, a few of the beautiful cathedrals.'

'Sounds like fun.' Lily responded with a smile.

And it was.

Examining the architectural masterpieces built several centuries ago, the exquisite workmanship created without machinery, the sense of ages past and the people who existed then, their lifestyles.

Lily became fascinated with the tales retold of high society passed down from generation to generation…undoubtedly a mixture of fable and truth.

There was a strong feeling of *belonging* that she found difficult to ignore, and she said as much.

'*Cara*, why not stay?' Sophia encouraged with apparent delight. 'You know how much I love having you with me.'

It would be so easy to say *yes*, and she caught hold of her aunt's hand and gave it a gentle squeeze. 'Let's discuss it over lunch.'

Sophia offered a sparkling smile. 'I know just the place.'

Indeed, Lily agreed a short while later as they entered a superbly decorated restaurant where the maître d' greeted Sophia by name.

Introductions complete, they were escorted to a table set with fine linen, quality cutlery and stem-ware.

Nice, she noted with pleasure, lovely ambience, exclusive fittings, well-spaced tables and chairs provided an overall elegance including the pleasant staff.

So far, so good, Lily accorded in silent approval, aware of the inevitability of comparison with her own and other eating establishments. Something, as a chef and restaurant owner, she found difficult not to do.

The menu also earned her respect, so too did the wine list for its superb selection.

Together they conferred, ordered and Lily met her aunt's interested gaze with a musing smile.

'I'd like to find restaurant work and lease a small apartment in Milan,' she intimated, and sought to explain her decision. 'I have an excellent manager and staff back home, and I'm confident Parisi will continue to operate to a high standard.'

Sophia's eyes sparkled as she clapped her hands. 'So you *are* going to stay. *Cara*, this is wonderful news.'

It was easy to offer a light laugh. 'I'm glad you approve.'

'How could I not?' Sophia lifted a hand, and the sommelier moved to their table. 'Wine, please. Today we celebrate.'

'Indeed,' Carlo agreed.

The wine was a superb Sauvignon Blanc, with which Sophia delivered a toast to Lily's Milanese sojourn, followed by a starter that proved a visual art form in presentation and taste. Surpassed, if it were possible, by the main. When it came to dessert, the exquisite meringue concoction defied description.

It was Lily who requested her compliments be relayed to the chef, the highly regarded Giovanni, whose name held a reverence superseded by few, according to Sophia.

Much to Lily's surprise he appeared at the close of their meal.

'Sophia. It is good to see you again,' he greeted with affection. 'You have a young friend with you today.'

'My niece and god-daughter, Lily,' Sophia relayed with a warm smile. 'Who is also a chef with her own restaurant in Sydney.'

'You are on holiday? Or do you intend to remain in Milan and find work immediately?'

She hadn't given too much thought to a timeframe. 'The latter.'

His interest appeared to quicken. 'Do you speak fluent Italian?'

'French, also,' Sophia enlightened. 'My niece spent a year in Paris studying French cuisine.'

'We are soon to close for a few hours. When you have finished your coffee, Giorgio, the maître d', will escort you to the kitchen, and we will talk.' He inclined his head. *'Scusi, per favore.'*

'It sounds promising, *cara*,' Sophia offered quietly. 'How would you feel if Giovanni offers you a position here?'

Take it, a silent voice prompted. 'Let's not get too excited until we've talked,' she said cautiously.

The coffee was rich, dark, aromatic, a perfect accompanying touch to end their meal.

It was then the maître d' approached their table to politely enquire if the lunch had met their satisfaction, and received gratifying assurance before he directed his attention to Lily.

'*Signorina*, if you are ready, I will escort you to the kitchen.'

Efficient was the first word that immediately came to mind as Lily entered the expansive workspace. Clean, uncluttered long stainless steel benches, good equipment, staff working well together, she noted in one sweeping glance.

Giovanni came forward and indicated a small office at the rear of the kitchen. 'We will talk in private.'

His queries focused on her training, where,

when, including her knowledge and experience. After which he showed her a variety of menus, whereupon they discussed ingredients, detailed methodology, in both Italian and French.

Testing her, she perceived, and she could only admire his professional approach.

'I require an assistant chef,' he explained. 'Would you be prepared to complete a one-day trial tomorrow?'

Tomorrow?

There was no room for hesitation. 'Yes.'

'Bene.' He mentioned hours and rate of pay. 'If you work well, the position is yours.' He stood and indicated the meeting was at an end. 'I shall expect you in the kitchen at seven in the morning.'

It was more than she'd hoped for. *Fate,* she rationalized as she rejoined Sophia and Carlo, and the benefit of being in the right place at the right time.

'It is yes, *sì*?' Sophia enquired at once, and Lily's smile said it all.

'Conditional on a one-day trial tomorrow,' she added, and found herself caught in an affectionate embrace.

'In which you will excel,' her aunt assured.

Such absolute certainty was touching, if a little premature. 'Possibly.' *Hopefully.*

'Lily, there can be no doubt,' Sophia gently chastised as she got to her feet. 'We need to collect whatever you will need for tomorrow,' her aunt decided as they exited the restaurant. 'Carlo will arrange accommodation for us in Milan overnight, and he will be available tomorrow to deliver you to and from the restaurant. Meantime I'll contact one of my friends who deals in the renting and leasing of real estate.'

'Whoa,' Lily protested with a cautionary gesture. 'First, let me get through tomorrow.'

'Of course.'

Sophia dalla Silvestri *on a roll* proved to be one very efficient woman as phone calls were made and received as Carlo returned them to Sophia's Lake Como villa, where Lily packed for an overnight stay and a full working day in Giovanni's kitchen.

'Alessandro has offered the use of his apartment,' Sophia relayed as Carlo negotiated evening traffic approaching the inner city streets of Milan.

You're kidding me. Lily carefully schooled her expression. 'How kind of him.'

'He doesn't expect to be in Milan until tomorrow.'

Please have him stay there overnight. The thought of sharing time and conducting polite conversation wasn't high on her list of favourite pastimes when she needed a good night's sleep.

Perhaps her plea was heeded, for there was no sign of him as she shared an evening meal with Sophia and Carlo...or when she retired to her guest suite.

Yet for some reason sleep appeared elusive, and despite the comfort of a luxurious bed, she tossed and turned, unable to still an active mind bent on a mental review of Giovanni's menus, matching ingredients with her own preferred method of preparation, while pondering if her work would meet his rigid standard.

Oh, give yourself a break, she mentally chastised as she listed her qualifications, experience, *knowledge.*

You'll be fine.

Sure she would, if only she could get some *sleep.*

Except after what seemed an endless amount of time, she threw aside the bedcovers, pulled a silk wrap over cotton sleep trousers and vest top, and made her way quietly downstairs to the kitchen.

A hot drink, calming meditative thoughts as she viewed the nightscape *had* to work.

The hot drink was fine...the meditative thoughts, not so much. As to the nightscape of twinkling street lights vying with coloured neon, the tracery of headlights from moving traffic made for minor distraction.

'Unable to sleep?'

Lily clutched her cup with both hands in an effort not to spill the remaining contents as she spared a startled glance at the man who moved to stand at her side.

Every nerve-end in her body sprang into alert as she sought to gather a semblance of calm. 'You're supposed to be in London.'

In the dim light Alessandro seemed taller, broader, somehow. He'd removed his jacket, his tie, and rolled back his shirt-sleeves. The casual look failed to detract from the masculine intensity he managed to exude without effort. 'I chose to return home.'

'To an empty bed at this late hour?' The words escaped before she gave them thought.

'Instead of a physically active night in a woman's arms?'

Lily's cheeks filled with warm heat, hopefully not visible in the dim light. 'If that's your pleasure,' she managed with a tinge of wry humour.

'You imagine I bed women indiscriminately, Liliana?'

His teasing use of her full name ignited something deep inside, a sensual flare that threatened to destroy her peace of mind. Even *thinking* about his powerful male body engaged in intimacy was enough to liquefy her bones.

'No comment,' she managed, as if it didn't matter to her in the slightest, and refused to admit on some deep level that it did.

His soft chuckle curled round her heart and squeezed a little. 'Beautiful, is it not?'

'The view?'

'Of course.'

So why did the unbidden thought occur that

it hadn't been the nightscape to which he'd referred?

'You are nervous of the day ahead?'

Of course he knew. If Carlo hadn't relayed the news, then Sophia undoubtedly had.

'A little,' she said with innate honesty, and sensed him move to stand behind her.

'Maybe this will help.'

His hands clasped her shoulders and began to knead the tense muscles, working them with an expertise that reefed a soft sigh from her throat.

It felt *good*. Dear heaven...so good. She closed her eyes, let her head roll forward, and simply gave in to his ministrations.

She shouldn't let him do this...shouldn't enjoy it so much.

Another minute, and I'll move away and bid him 'goodnight'.

She did...although it was *three* minutes, not one.

And it was *she* who felt bereft as he trailed light fingers down her cheek as she stood momentarily transfixed before she sought to escape.

Alessandro watched her with narrowed eyes and reflected what her reaction might have been if he'd pulled her close and taken her mouth on his own…as he'd been strongly tempted to do.

Lily's initial reservations were soon dispelled as she was introduced to the kitchen staff, shown where the various cooking implements were located, the contents of the pantry, the cold storeroom…and familiarized herself with the lunch menu.

Beneath Giovanni's initial supervision, she prepared, diced, sliced poultry, veal, vegetables and tended to the making of fresh pasta.

Concentration and attention to detail kept her focused, and she worked with quick diligence, enjoying the adrenalin surge as the restaurant opened its doors for lunch, and the pace increased dramatically as kitchen staff plated up orders, checked, ready to be collected by the waiters and waitresses on duty and served.

Teamwork at a premium, Lily accorded, discovering Giovanni to be a hard, but fair, taskmaster who didn't hold back if he declared a dish didn't reach his standard of perfection.

Fortunately, to her immense relief, no harsh words were directed at her.

Once the desserts were plated, the pressure began to ease.

As the final few clientele departed and the restaurant doors closed, there was time for the ongoing clean-up to restore the kitchen to its former state, a break for kitchen and wait-staff alike, before the need to prepare the evening dinner menu.

Lily earned a discerning nod of approval from Giovanni, and an introduction to the wait-staff, one of whom was an attractive blonde girl in her early twenties from the UK, named Hannah, whose deep blue eyes twinkled with mischievous humour.

The break included a light meal, coffee, then it became necessary to work the kitchen in preparation for the dinner patrons.

Lunch was a walk in the park compared to dinner, which rated among the busiest Lily had experienced in a long time. It reminded her of her sojourn in Paris, with voluble directions uttered by tense kitchen staff when even the slightest delay arose in plating up orders.

Yet it was familiar territory, one around which

she'd structured her life and enjoyed, even if it tended to frazzle the nerves on occasion.

However the sense of achievement and satisfaction overrode any temporary moments when things went haywire.

It was late, almost midnight when she removed her apron and cap, and tossed them in the laundry bin.

She checked her cell-phone and opened a text message alerting a car was waiting outside for her.

Giovanni approached her as she collected her bag.

'The position is yours. You will alternate between the lunch and dinner shifts. Beginning Monday you'll be on lunch shift to start with. Start time the same as this morning.' He paused a moment, then offered a faint smile. 'You work well.'

Her heart lifted a little. 'Thank you.'

'Buona notte.'

Most of the kitchen staff had already left, and Lily lifted a hand to the two who remained before she exited through the side door.

The sleek car was parked close by and she

breathed a sigh of relief as a tall dark figure emerged from behind the wheel and crossed to open the passenger door.

Thank you, Lily breathed silently. A smooth ride to Alessandro's apartment, a leisurely hot shower, then bed.

She was so caught up with the vision she didn't immediately notice it was Alessandro, and not Carlo, who held open the door.

He saw the moment she realized *who* had driven to collect her, glimpsed the way her body stilled for a few seconds before she stepped past him and slid into the passenger seat.

'Carlo was unavailable?'

Alessandro bit back a wry smile as he crossed to take his position behind the wheel and turned towards her. 'You would have preferred his company?'

'He is easy to talk to.'

'And I am not?'

He held her gaze as she met his own, and wondered if she knew how well he could read her.

'No.'

A slight smile curved his mouth. 'Indeed? Perhaps you'd care to elaborate?'

She gave him a sweet smile. 'No.'

He watched as she leaned her head against the headrest, and sensed her slight sigh as he ignited the engine and eased the car onto the road.

'Tough day?'

'Giovanni hired me.'

But he'd put her through her paces. Doubtless she was accustomed to long days in a restaurant of her own, but in a strange kitchen with unfamiliar staff, it would have been more taxing.

'This is what you want?'

'Yes.' It provided a reason for her to stay awhile, and that was a *good* thing, Lily rationalized as the car purred through illuminated streets.

Oncoming traffic briefly highlighted the hard planes of Alessandro's facial features, and she became conscious of his hands on the wheel as he handled the road.

There was a latent strength apparent that touched a nerve deep inside…something she attempted to dismiss, and failed.

Once she gained her independence, she'd probably hardly see him at all.

So why did that leave her feeling vaguely bereft?

Tomorrow she'd enlist Sophia's help and they'd arrange to check out apartments, and shop. She'd need sheets, towels. A car, she added silently. Public transport after the lunch shift would be OK, but late at night? Although there was always a cab...

Lily became so caught up with a *to do* list it came as a surprise to realize the car had slid to a halt adjacent Alessandro's apartment building.

The lift transported them swiftly to the designated level, where she preceded him into the softly lit apartment before turning to face him.

'Thank you.'

She was pale, her eyes darkened with a fatigue she fought hard to control. He should extend a polite acknowledgement, and let her go upstairs to her suite.

'So...thank me.' His voice was a husky drawl, and he saw her eyes dilate.

The air grew heavy...*charged,* almost dangerous, and he caught the increased pulse-beat at the base of her throat. He cupped her chin and traced his thumb pad along the fullness of her lower lip, applied light pressure to its centre, then he trailed a gentle path to settle on the fast-beating pulse.

For a moment she lost all thought, aware on some level that this shouldn't be happening, yet caught up with the unbidden need to lift her arms around his neck and press her body close in against his own.

Shocked dismay brought a return of sanity as she stepped back in a silent bid to put some distance between them.

He let her go, and she stood transfixed, caught in the thrall of sensual awareness.

It irked that he knew. Worse, that he observed her struggle for composure. Words she wanted to fling at him remained locked in her throat for a few long seconds, then she tilted her head and met his narrowed gaze.

'Don't play with me, Alessandro.'

Alessandro remained silent, his dark eyes steady as they locked with her own.

'I'm not playing.'

He saw her eyes widen with a degree of uncertainty, and pressed home the advantage as he lowered his head and took possession of her mouth.

Gentle at first, teasing, exploring a little as he tempted her response. The need to deepen the kiss was overwhelming, and he ached to pull her in to the cradle of his hips, shape her to his body.

He could, easily...but at what cost?

For two decades he'd trusted his instinct, prior to which his life had been totally dependent on a deeply ingrained gut feeling that had saved him from grievous injury, or worse.

Too much too soon, and he might lose.

With considerable restraint he lightened his touch, lingered a little as he traced the generous curve of her mouth with his own, then he lifted his head and brushed a soft caress to her temple before releasing his hold.

For a heart-wrenching moment she looked lost, almost adrift, then she turned away from him, crossed the room and ascended the stairs without so much as a backward glance.

Sleep proved elusive, as Lily tossed and turned in bed in an attempt to dispel Alessandro's forceful image, his touch, the sweet sorcery of his kiss. And the way he made her *feel*.

At odds with herself, *him*, and, admit it, torn between desire and the need to contain it.

She wanted a calm, carefree lifestyle. Hadn't she travelled to Italy to seek just that? No way did she want to be caught up in an emotional whirlpool.

She needed to focus on the positives. A new life, new position, and within days she'd have an apartment and her own car.

Mercifully it was the last thing she remembered as sleep claimed her.

CHAPTER FIVE

ANOTHER email from James resided in her inbox when Lily checked her laptop early the next morning.

Not so pleasant was his message stating if he didn't hear from her within forty-eight hours he intended to talk to her in person.

Her fingers flew as she keyed in a 'don't waste your time' response and hit 'Reply'.

Did he *really* think she'd overlook his *temporary distraction* and accept him back into her life?

It only proved he didn't know her at all, Lily consoled as she moved downstairs and felt a sense of relief on discovering Sophia was the sole occupant of the dining room.

Pretending normality in Alessandro's presence after his fateful claim last night would have considerably affected her composure.

'Alessandro has already left, but not before he relayed you are to begin work in the restaurant next week. I am delighted for you.' Sophia's eyes sparkled with pleasure.

Lily found it easy to smile as she poured coffee into her cup, added sugar, and savoured the aromatic liquid. 'Thank you. I'm pleased it worked out OK.'

'You will need to be settled by the weekend,' Sophia offered with a degree of concern. 'Today Carlo will take us to my friend's agency and we will look at apartments, *sì*?'

'Please,' she accepted gratefully. 'That would be great.'

'*Bene*. Now tell me about yesterday while you eat, then we will leave.'

Sophia and her friend, Julia, proved a knowledgeable pair as they selected suitable locations, rental availability and together they set out with an intent to view.

There were a few provisos. Sophia insisted the apartment must be in a good locale, comfortably furnished with excellent security and parking facilities.

Julia proved to be very thorough, her recommendations valid as she took them through no less than five apartments, any one of which Lily would have been happy to lease.

'We shall have lunch,' Sophia declared as they exited the fifth apartment. 'Then we continue our viewing.'

'Excellent idea,' Julia agreed. 'I think you will be pleased with a particular one I have in mind.'

'Saving the best for last?' Lily quizzed, and earned a light laugh in return.

'It is business, *sì*? Besides, today provides me the opportunity to spend time with a dear friend, and enjoy the pleasure of meeting her beloved god-daughter.'

It was Julia who chose the restaurant and insisted on playing hostess, while Lily listened to their light-hearted banter with the maître d', deferring to each other over what to order and whether they would indulge in wine.

Two apartments were on the afternoon's agenda to view, and it was the second of the two that clinched the deal for Lily.

Situated in a lovely street, the building itself had been restored and renovated while adhering to a classic style. Comfortable, extremely functional, with a medium-size lounge, an en suite adjoining the main bedroom as well as a separate bathroom for the guest bedroom. Utilities were modern, and the kitchen and dining room were warm and inviting. Fully furnished, the apartment had security and off-street parking. Added to which the lease provided flexibility and the rental was reasonable.

'This is the one,' Lily declared with a delighted smile. 'I'll take it.'

Sophia and Julia clapped their hands with pleasure.

'Good. You do not require time to consider?'

She shook her head in immediate negation. 'No.' Her smile said it all as she turned towards Julia. 'You have the relevant paperwork available?'

'At my office,' Julia enlightened. 'We will head there now.'

There was a sense of satisfaction in signing the lease, for to achieve employment *and* an apartment within a few short days seemed incredible.

The next acquisition would be the purchase of her own transport. And sheets, towels, a few items to personalize the apartment.

'You are deep in thought,' Sophia observed as Carlo returned them to her villa in Como, and Lily reached across the rear passenger seat to link her fingers within Sophia's own.

'Thank you.'

'*Cara*, whatever for?'

'Everything,' she said with warm simplicity, and felt the slight pressure as Sophia curled Lily's fingers within her own.

'My dear, I have a vested interest in your happiness, as well as a personal desire to have you with me for as long as possible.'

The warmth of familial love struck a sensitive chord, and Lily swallowed the sudden lump that rose in her throat. Tears were close to the surface, and she quickly blinked to dispel them—she didn't *do* the crying thing.

The insistent burr of her cell-phone had her reaching into her bag to extract it and she felt her stomach tighten as she recognized the number displayed, despite deleting James's name from her caller ID register.

Without a qualm she simply closed the phone, thereby cutting the connection only to have the call repeated.

This time she let it ring out, which incurred Sophia's questioning look, and Lily shook her head.

'I'll deal with the call later.'

Hopefully James would *get* the message she had no intention of having contact with him ever again.

Apparently not so, for Carlo had just drawn the car to a halt adjacent the entrance to Sophia's villa when the phone rang again.

Lily stepped out from the car, extracted the phone, and felt the anger build as she viewed the familiar number.

OK, so he was being deliberately obtuse.

'Do not email or attempt to call me,' she voiced with chilling resolve. 'It's over. Finished.'

'Lily, darling, please listen to me—'

Not in this millennium. 'There is no point.' She cut the connection and closed the phone.

'Problems, *cara*?' Sophia queried with concern, and Lily shook her head.

'Nothing I can't handle.'

Hopefully now her ex-fiancé would had finally got the message...

A leisurely shower helped take her mind off

it, so too did a light evening meal, after which she shared a glass of wine with Sophia as they discussed plans for the next day, firmed them, before mutually choosing to retire.

It was surprising what could be achieved within a short space of time, Lily reflected as Carlo stored the second, no, *third* assortment of packages into the trunk of Sophia's car.

Almost every item on her list was accounted for, and there was an enormous degree of plea-sure in knowing only *one* item remained…a car.

By far the most expensive, and fortified by a leisurely lunch Carlo despatched them to a car dealership where, after some skillful haggling of her own, she purchased a funky silver model, perfectly suitable for her needs.

'Well done,' Carlo accorded quietly as Sophia enfolded her in a congratulatory hug.

'Thank you.' Payment was organized, her in-ternational driving licence scrutinized, insur-ance arranged and the car was ready to be driven away.

'Let's get this babe on the road,' Lily said, and laughed as she offered Carlo a high-five gesture, then she slid behind the wheel and followed his car to her apartment.

Home, for however long she chose to make it her own, Lily decided with pleasure as they transferred the day's purchases into the second bedroom.

All that remained was the need to transfer her belongings from Sophia's villa tomorrow.

Something that was achieved with mixed emotions the next day as Lily and her aunt shared an affectionate hug as Sophia and Carlo departed Lily's apartment.

'I shall miss having you stay with me,' Sophia voiced with sincere regret. 'But knowing you are so close is a joy, for we will see each other often.' She brightened considerably. 'There is the Charity Gala on Saturday evening. It will be a wonderful event.' She brushed her lips to Lily's cheek. 'We will collect you at eight.'

'*Grazie, Zia.* I couldn't have achieved any of this without your help.' She caught her aunt close in an affectionate hug. 'Once I know my work roster, I'll organize an evening to invite you to dinner. Carlo, too.' Her eyes took on a humorous sparkle. 'I'll make something special.'

'That will be lovely, *cara*. I assume the invitation will include Alessandro?'

Lily didn't so much as blink. 'Naturally.'

There was a brief 'ohmygod, what have I done?' moment as Lily watched Sophia leave with Carlo at the wheel.

When it came to entertaining, two guests or three made little difference.

Except when it included a man who sent her emotions into a panic whenever she was in his presence.

So deal with it.

With determination she turned from the window and began unpacking.

It didn't take long, and afterwards she made a few changes, aligning a sofa to a more comfortable angle, sorting through kitchen cupboards and, importantly, making a list of food she needed to purchase.

It was late when she finally slid into bed.

Tomorrow she intended shopping for personal touches to make the apartment more *her*, and she fell asleep halfway through picturing various images in her mind…an ornament she'd sighted in a shop window, an alarm clock, and a large colourful cushion that would be perfect.

The next few days passed in a blur of shopping and exploring at will, adding touches to the apartment, changing a few things to her taste.

The Charity Gala meant dress-up time, and Lily viewed her gown's sheer style in pale shades of pink, blue and lavender silk chiffon with a pleased eye, for it flattered her slender curves and fell in a soft swirl at her ankles. A delicate wrap in matching silk chiffon added a finishing touch, and lavender stilettos completed the outfit.

A timeless design she'd fallen in love with at first sight, and, as Sophia had assured, perfect to wear to the fund-raising gala scheduled for this evening.

In five minutes the in-house phone would ring heralding Sophia and Carlo's arrival, and Lily used the time to run a last-minute check of her hair and make-up… She was good to go.

Right on cue, the phone pealed, she caught up her purse and took the lift down to the lobby. The doors slid apart to reveal Alessandro standing a few feet distant looking, she saw at a glance, far too ruggedly attractive for any woman's peace of mind.

Especially her own.

Attired in a black evening suit that had to be tailored specifically to mould his breadth of shoulder and hard-muscled frame, white linen and black bow tie, he resembled a photographic male model.

Yet no photograph could reveal the element of arresting power he exuded, or the primitive sensuality that was his alone.

Dangerous...a hungry lover capable of driving a woman beyond reason.

Dear Lord in heaven...where had that come from?

Smile, Lily bade as she sought to control her wayward imagination. *Step forward...speak!*

'Hi,' she managed with measured politeness. 'I expected to see Sophia and Carlo.'

Did she glimpse a faint gleam of humour in his dark eyes before it was quickly masked?

'Carlo is delivering Sophia directly to the venue.'

'And sent you in his stead. It's very kind of you.'

One eyebrow lifted a little. 'So polite, Lily?'

'I was aiming for *gracious*.'

His husky laugh sent the blood coursing through her veins, and she deliberately widened her eyes.

'I guess I failed.'

'Miserably,' Alessandro agreed as he indicated his car parked immediately adjacent the entrance. 'Shall we leave?'

It was, Lily accorded with a masked degree of awe, an incredible gathering of guests as she entered the large historic venue at Alessandro's side.

Beautifully restored splendour lent a timeless aura to a modern event. Genuine artworks graced the expansive foyer, while the huge ballroom bore exquisite sconces, suspended chandeliers gave the illusion of light, enhanced by cleverly concealed electric bulbs to provide added illumination.

There had been several occasions when she'd attended charity fund-raiser events with her parents, but nothing on the scale of this evening's affair.

Refined elegance seemed a perfect description, and it didn't take much imagination to reflect on a former era of fashionable balls with members of the Italian and foreign royalty in attendance.

'This place is really something,' Lily said quietly, and incurred Alessandro's musing look.

'It appeals to you?'

'How could it not?'

'Alessandro. *Caro.*'

It wasn't the two words so much, but the cadence in the feminine voice which uttered them. *Seductive* didn't quite cover it, Lily decided as she turned slightly to see if the voice matched the woman.

Oh, my. In spades…and then some.

For even to the most jaundiced eye, the woman who moved to Alessandro's side was a vision of perfection from her raven black wavy hair to the tips of her shoes. Beautiful facial features cleverly accented with skilfully applied cosmetics, gleaming dark, almost black, eyes, and a figure to die for clothed in what had to be a designer original. The right touch with jewellery, expensive but not ostentatious.

Definitely the *wow* factor.

'Giarda.' Alessandro's greeting held warm affection and Lily offered a polite smile, only to freeze as he curved an arm around her waist. 'I'd like you to meet Liliana.'

Not *Lily, Sophia's niece,* just...*Liliana,* And why did her birth name sound so *sexy* as it fell from his lips?

'Giarda is married to one of my business colleagues,' he explained, and Giarda offered a light laugh.

'Alessandro and my husband vied with each other for me.' Her eyes twinkled with mischief. 'Massimo won.'

'How...nice.' What else could she say?

'For me, yes. Not so for Alessandro.'

'I'm sure he recovered,' Lily managed with a touch of humour, and Giarda inclined her head.

'Of course,' Giarda acknowledged with a warm smile. 'We remain the best of friends.' She turned towards Alessandro. 'It pleases me to see you attached to such a charming young woman. You must bring Lily to dinner. I will be in touch to determine a mutually suitable evening.'

'Thank you.'

Lily waited until Giarda was out of earshot before facing him. 'I am not *your* young woman.'

'You left out *charming.*'

'Then there's the touchy-feely thing.' Her eyes flashed. 'I refuse to act as arm candy.'

He regarded her with interest. 'You imagine I would use you as such?'

'Oh, *please.*'

'So unsure of your appeal, Lily?' Alessandro queried gently.

The air between them became electrifying, and for a few seemingly long seconds everything faded from her vision as she became caught up with a host of conflicting emotions.

Her relationship with James had been comfortable, pleasant, she admitted. Or so she'd imagined.

Yet Alessandro aroused a primitive passion deep within that made her yearn for the impossible.

There was a part of her that wanted to discard any reservations and simply enjoy what he offered for however long it might last.

Except that would be akin to treading a certain path to emotional self-destruction. Not something anyone in their right mind would willingly seek.

Alessandro took in the fast-thudding pulse at the base of her throat, and resisted the temptation to trace the hollow with a gentle finger. Yet here, now, was neither the time or place.

'Alessandro. Lily.'

Whatever he might have said didn't find voice as they turned in unison to greet Sophia.

'I am a little late,' Sophia explained as she brushed Lily's cheek with her own. 'Carlo was caught up in traffic.' She stood back a little and regarded Lily with affectionate approval. '*Cara*, you look stunning.'

'Beautiful,' Alessandro added as he took Lily's hand and brought it to his lips.

Her eyes dilated as they met his dark gleaming gaze only to attempt to make light of his gesture by offering a winsome smile.

'I believe every available ticket has sold,' Sophia revealed as she accepted a flute of champagne from one of the many waiters circling the room. 'Guests tend to be generous when the funds being raised benefit terminally ill children.'

A request for guests to be seated as dinner was about to be served ensured a general move towards numbered tables, and Lily bore Alessandro's light touch at the edge of her waist as he escorted them to their table.

Shared by fellow guests, among whom were Giarda and her husband Massimo—an attractive man whose dark features held a similar degree of ruthless power on a par with Alessandro's.

They had fought for Giarda's attention and Alessandro had accorded Massimo *colleague*, but were they friends in business, or adversaries? Lily posed as they took their seats.

A certain mutual respect became evident, she decided as the evening progressed. Alessandro was seated between Sophia and herself, with Massimo and Giarda opposite. The remaining five guests comprised a middle-aged couple, their son and two daughters.

Throughout the three-course dinner the eldest of the two daughters did her best to engage Alessandro's attention, which to give him credit, he fielded with polite charm.

Lily silently assured she didn't care and knew she lied. Which in itself was a conundrum, given the state of her emotions were in direct contrast to the dictates of her mind.

Come Monday she'd be involved with work, back in a kitchen, where she wanted to be. Social activities involving Alessandro's presence would dwindle to almost nothing.

Not before time. She'd done *complicated*, now all she wanted was routine and a simple lifestyle.

The fund-raiser was announced as an outstanding success as individual donations brought the total raised beyond expectations.

Gradually the guests began to leave, pausing to chat with friends and consequently progress into the foyer became slow.

It had been sufficiently disturbing to be seated close to Alessandro throughout the evening; somehow it seemed even more so to have his arm resting loosely at her waist during their passage from ballroom to foyer.

An action Lily attempted to convince herself was merely a courtesy and failed, for there was a sense of *rightness* in the contact, and although she vigorously denied it she felt...*what? Protected*. Which was insane.

In the name of heaven, *get real*. Blame the champagne, although she'd merely sipped the contents from one flute.

Within a few minutes she'd slip into the car

with Sophia, and Carlo would deliver her to her apartment.

Except when Sophia's car drew level with the entrance it was Sophia who bade them both *buona notte* and slid into the rear seat, leaving Lily almost speechless as Carlo eased the large vehicle forward into the steady stream of departing traffic.

'I'll get a taxi.' The words left her lips with stiff resolve, and all it achieved was Alessandro's studied inspection.

'That won't be necessary.'

'I wouldn't dream of taking you out of your way.'

He indicated his sleek black car sliding to a halt adjacent the entrance. 'Let's go.'

Lily spared a look of muted defiance, and her eyes widened as he leant in close. 'Do you really want to argue?'

She caught the flashbulbs of eager paparazzi, foreseeing how her reluctance would appear on celluloid, and she slid into the passenger seat with a forced smile, which she maintained until Alessandro cleared the venue and entered the main stream of traffic.

'I could easily have summoned a taxi.'

'Not unless you chose to wait in line for up to an hour or more. Something I would refuse to allow you to do.'

She opened her mouth to verbally damn him, only to close it again.

Silence seemed the best option, and she maintained it until Alessandro drew the car to a halt outside the entrance to her apartment building.

With undue haste she released her seat belt and reached for the door clasp, only to have him cut the engine and step out from the car.

'Thank you for the ride home.'

The external lighting accented his profile as he stood tall, like a dark angel for a few measurable seconds before he crossed to her side and held out his hand.

'I'll see you indoors.'

Lily tilted her head and threw him a dark look. 'It isn't necessary.'

His eyes speared her own, and with slow deliberation he cradled her face and lowered his head to capture her mouth with his own.

For a stark moment she became helplessly caught up in the sensual magic of his touch. A soft groan rose in her throat as she wavered between kissing him back or attempting to move away, instinctively aware she should take the latter action if she wanted to preserve her emotional sanity.

Except...*ohmygod*, he was good at this. *Far too good*.

A kiss...it was just a kiss.

Yet it became more, almost as if he was intent on staking a claim.

The temptation to wind her arms around his neck became difficult to resist, and she leaned in, threading her fingers through his hair as she kissed him back, loving the way his tongue stroked her own, teasing a little in an erotic dance that drove her wild.

She wanted to touch him, skin on skin, so she could explore his hard-muscled body. To nibble a little, taste and savour until he groaned and sought more; to become lost, beyond rational thought as she indulged in the release sex would provide.

Except that was all it would be...sex. And she didn't do one-night stands. Or sex without commitment.

Worse, what in hell was she *thinking*?

Two months ago she'd caught James *in flagrante delicto*, and vowed never to place her trust in another man ever again.

*So…*chill. *Stop this* now, *before it gets out of hand.*

Alessandro sensed the moment she began to withdraw, and he lightened his touch, sliding his hands up her arms to cradle her face as his mouth lingered a little, caressing the soft swollen contours before he slowly raised his head to search her features.

Eyes dark with passion, cheeks slightly heated, the faint quiver of her lips, and the edges of his mouth lifted a little in a gentle smile as he caught hold of her hand.

'I'll see you to your apartment, then leave.'

He crossed to the lift, pressed the call button and when the doors slid open he led her inside.

Lily didn't offer a word as they reached her floor, nor did she object when he took the key from her nerveless fingers and unlocked her apartment door.

Seconds later he handed her the key and gently pushed her inside.

'*Buona notte*, Lily.'

The door closed, and she automatically deactivated the alarm system, then she crossed into her bedroom, discarded her clothes, pulled on sleepwear, and slipped into bed to lie awake into the early hours of the morning.

CHAPTER SIX

'Two veal parmigiana, one salad, one steamed vegetables,' Lily read, and she began plating up the order for Hannah to collect and serve.

Day two on the lunch shift, and the restaurant was almost at full capacity.

Giovanni, the head chef, was a tough but fair taskmaster, ensuring the food chain worked at maximum efficiency.

Very little, if anything, escaped him, his eagle eye known to catch the smallest imperfection.

Ego didn't exist in his kitchen, although Cristo, the second chef, while not verbally temperamental, could on occasion lift his hands in the air and throw the darkest of looks at anyone who dared get in his way.

Lily loved the energy necessary to prepare the day's menu… The delicate sauces for the various pasta dishes. The exquisite desserts that re-sembled a visual work of art.

Food—watching her parents select the best quality, prepare, cook and present it—formed her earliest memories, developing her own creativity with the need to explore, experiment, study at home and abroad, in a bid to perfect her expertise in the art of cuisine.

Osso buco was next up, and Lily plated up, added spinach and pine nuts drizzled with olive oil, together with toasted *ciabatta*.

Any time soon the orders for mains would dwindle, and be replaced by dessert orders, fol-lowed by coffee. By mid-afternoon she'd be able to toss her apron in the laundry bin and finish for the day.

Just as she was about to do so she heard Giovanni call her name, and she turned as he moved to her side.

'Cristo has a family emergency. Can you work his shift this evening?'

She didn't hesitate. 'No problem.'

Together they went through the dinner menu, Cristo's work was re-assigned, and Lily checked the large pantry and cold room.

Busy didn't cover it as the restaurant began to fill with evening clientele, and deft speed became essential as the wait-staff presented order after order for the kitchen staff to fill.

The need to work well together became paramount, and Lily did what she did best, worked under pressure by focusing on what needed to be done.

There were a few moments of light relief as Hannah's sense of humour came to the fore.

'Canadian on table five isn't happy with his steak.' She achieved an impressive eye-roll. 'Medium rare in Canada is *not* what we served him. He wants the meat pink with a red-blood centre. No oozing blood, but close.'

A fussy customer needed to be a happy customer. 'OK.' Lily fired up the grill, cut a fresh beef fillet, seared, checked and plated it. 'Good to go. With the chef's compliments.'

Within minutes Hannah reappeared to collect another order. 'Success. Although he would have preferred *Canadian* beef.'

'Really?'

'*Really*. I very politely explained the restaurant only bought the finest beef from a hill farm owned by a caring family whose stock was personally hand fed.'

Lily's eyes gleamed as she tamped down the urge to laugh. 'You didn't.'

'Uh-huh. He appeared impressed.' Hannah collected the order and sailed back to the restaurant.

The pace was fast, and it was good to reach the late evening plateau where most of the customers had moved on from their main course and were content to linger over dessert and coffee.

It was almost the end of the evening shift when Giorgio, the maître d', entered the kitchen and crossed to Lily's side.

'There is a gentleman who wishes to speak with you.'

She cast him a look of surprise. 'Did he give you his name?'

'James. Signor James.'

Her *ex*? Ex-fiancé, ex-friend…ex-everything?

James? *Here* in Milan, at *this* particular restaurant? *You have to be joking?*

Coincidence didn't stretch that far.

While it wouldn't have been difficult for him to connect her to Sophia, there was no way her aunt would divulge where Lily lived or worked. Yet somehow James had managed to find out, and for some reason, he'd decided to board a flight to Italy and force a personal confrontation.

Hell...the silent curse stuck in her throat.

Like she needed this?

Calm, she could do calm, and she offered Giorgio a wry look. 'The man is an ex-fiancé and no longer a friend of mine.'

'You do not want to speak with him?'

'Please. If you don't mind.'

Giorgio inclined his head, and Lily returned her attention to plating up an order, unaware the maître d' slipped into the private office and made a phone call before returning to the front desk.

Hopefully James would accept the relayed words and leave.

Yet there was a certain degree of trepidation as she dispensed with her apron and bade the remaining kitchen staff goodnight.

Surely James wouldn't wait for her?

Except there he was, standing at the edge of the pavement as she exited the restaurant, making it impossible for her to avoid him.

With long strides he moved towards her and

attempted to take her hands in his own, swiftly she locked them together behind her back.

'James,' Lily acknowledged stiffly. 'What are you doing here?'

'To convince you, in person, that I made the biggest mistake of my life.' He spread his hands in a helpless gesture. 'Emails and phone calls weren't achieving anything.'

What could she say that she hadn't relayed verbally at the time, and later via email?

'Our relationship was over the moment I walked into my home and discovered you in bed with another woman.'

'It didn't mean anything.' He took a step closer. 'I was a fool. Please give me a second chance,' he implored with desperation. 'I love you.'

She doubted he ever had.

'We've done this. Let's not do it again.'

'Lily—'

'Just…go, James.'

'Lily, I'm begging you. *Please.*'

She didn't see it coming and she *should* have, as he pulled her close and brought his mouth down on hers with a hungry force that stunned and sickened her as she fought to free herself.

With a deep-throated growl she kicked him *hard* and took advantage of his momentary surprise to wrench away from him.

'Don't touch me, you...*imbecile*.' She wiped a hand over her mouth and glared at him in a manner that spoke volumes. 'If you come near me again, I'll have you arrested for harassment.'

'You can't be serious.'

'Very.' Succinct and vehement.

He went to reach for her again...and this time Lily was ready for him.

'Don't.'

'I suggest you take Lily's advice,' a deep, slightly accented *familiar* voice drawled, and she swung around to face Alessandro leaning against his gleaming black car parked at the kerb.

How long had he been standing there?

Lily tilted her chin as she regarded his inscrutable features. 'I can manage this.'

'Of that I have no doubt,' Alessandro concurred in a silky drawl that sent shivers scudding down her spine.

James, however, directed Alessandro a resentful glare. 'This is between me and my fiancée and none of your business.'

'*Ex-fiancée*,' Lily corrected at once. 'As of almost two months ago.'

'We're working at reconciling.'

'There is no *we*,' she assured with considerable force.

'And no chance of a reconciliation...*ever*.'

Alessandro switched his attention to James. 'A definite *no*, wouldn't you agree?'

'She doesn't know what she wants,' James declared in a dismissive tone, and failed to notice the tension edge up a notch.

'It doesn't appear to be you.'

'Really?' James spared him a hard look. 'And you are?'

'A friend.'

James turned to Lily and indicated a compact hire car. 'I'll follow you home, and we can talk in private.'

Alessandro searched Lily's features. 'Is that what you want?'

He reminded her of a panther, waiting, watchful, and dangerous.

'No,' she replied without hesitation, and saw him turn towards James.

'I suggest you leave,' he indicated silkily.

'Or you'll do *what*?' James demanded tren-chantly.

Alessandro didn't move so much as a muscle. Yet only a fool would ignore the coiled strength apparent in his stance. 'Ensure you never forget my name.'

James took in the expensive suit, the indisput-able air of power, the luxury car and looked at Lily with bitter anger.

'You *owe* me.'

She met his gaze squarely. 'I owe you nothing.' He'd lived in her home, for which she had paid all the bills, maintenance, even groceries. Not to mention forfeiting deposits paid on the wed-ding reception venue, florist, limousines, honey-moon... The list was endless.

James hands clenched into tight fists, and for a moment Lily thought he meant to launch a physi-cal attack. Then without a further word he moved to his car, slid in behind the wheel, and drove off with a roar of the engine and fast-spinning wheels.

Lily took a moment before she turned to face the inimitable man who stood regarding her with masked interest.

'You, of course, just *happened* to be passing by.'

'I was in the neighborhood.'

She looked at him with a degree of scepticism. 'You expect me to believe that?'

'Does it matter?'

His scrutiny intensified when she didn't answer, and her eyes widened as he cupped her chin and tilted her head.

Her mouth felt slightly numb from James's onslaught, and without thought she soothed her swollen lower lip with the edge of her tongue.

Alessandro bit back a barely audible oath as he drew her close. She touched something deep inside him, a need for *one* special woman in his life. *Family* of his own, children. *Love*, the true abiding kind, from which he'd considered himself immune. Until now.

A faintly wry smile curved his generous mouth as she tucked her head into the curve of his shoulder and rested there for a few seemingly long minutes.

Unbidden, he slid a hand to her nape, then slowly smoothed it down her back.

She fitted so well, almost as if she was meant

to be there, and he lowered his head to brush his lips to her temple, ignoring his instinct to put her in his car and take her home…to *his* home.

Not an option, yet. And he experienced a measure of regret as she stepped away from him.

Alessandro retrieved his wallet, extracted a card and handed it to her. 'My cell-phone number. Any problems, call me. Understood?'

'Thank you.' Lily pocketed the card. 'Goodnight, Alessandro.'

He trailed light fingers down her cheek. 'Drive carefully.'

She inclined her head, and he watched as she crossed to her car, waiting until she disappeared from sight before easing away from the kerb.

To pass Lily's apartment building in order to reach his own involved little effort on his part, and he swung by, relieved to see she was safely indoors, with no sign of her ex-fiancé's hired car anywhere in sight.

A text message to Sophia on his arrival home would ease her concern following James's enquiry as to Lily's whereabouts. Giorgio's awareness of the situation was an added benefit.

* * *

Lily spent a restless night as James's pleading words and empty promises echoed in her mind. Not the least of which that he'd sought to lodge an appeal in person, given she had made in perfectly clear their relationship was dead and buried. How could he possibly imagine she might consider a reconciliation? Why would any woman in her right mind go ahead with a wedding on discovering her fiancé had been conducting a long-running affair behind her back?

Please.

Eventually she must have fallen asleep, for she woke as the dawn fingered through her bedroom shutters, and she rose, dressed, drank strong coffee, enjoyed a leisurely breakfast, then she made the call to reassure Sophia and soothe her aunt's concern.

Alessandro in the guise of white knight wasn't mentioned, while the need to change her cell-phone number to a private listing became paramount.

Effecting the change involved a personal application, form-filling, presentation of required documentation, but eventually she was given a new number. Something she fitted in before and after her lunch shift at the restaurant.

Her list of things to do completed, she arrived home, as she was beginning to regard the apartment, as the sun sat low in the sky, and just as she set her bag on the kitchen counter her cell-phone rang.

Sophia…had to be, as her aunt was the only person to whom she'd given her new number.

'Lily, I'm so pleased I caught you. Alessandro requests you call him in connection with arrangements to dine with Giarda and Massimo tomorrow evening. I believe you have his cell-phone number?'

'I do.'

'*Ciao,* darling. Be careful.'

Of whom? Lily queried silently. James or Alessandro? A hollow laugh rose to the surface. Each man was equally dangerous. Just in a different way.

Purchases unpacked, she retrieved her cell-phone and Alessandro's card, then she dialled his number.

He picked up on the fifth ring, his voice crisp as he intoned, 'Del Marco.'

'Lily,' she reciprocated. 'Sophia relayed a message for me to call you.' She paused fractionally. 'Is this a good time?'

'If you count standing dripping wet and naked, having just stepped from the shower,' Alessandro drawled.

There was a second's silence. 'I'll call back.' Then she cut the connection, and released the pent-up breath caused by a vivid vision of his tall muscular frame sans clothes. Dripping wet.

Not good for her heart rate. Or her equilibrium as heat pooled deep within causing provocative images she found unsettling. *Very* unsettling.

So go do *something,* Lily chided, and she withdrew the vacuum cleaner from a storage cupboard. *Cleaning* was good. After which she'd shower, dress in comfortable clothes, prepare dinner, *then* she'd call back.

An hour and a half went by before she picked up the phone and keyed in his number.

'Lily.'

Alessandro acknowledged with a hint of amusement, and his mouth curved as she queried drily, 'You're not in the middle of anything?'

'At the moment…no.'

'You wanted to contact me,' she prompted.

'Before we continue, give me your new number.'

She did, and she checked each one as he repeated them.

'I'll collect you at seven thirty tomorrow evening. We're meeting Giarda and Massimo at eight.'

'I can meet you there.'

'But you won't.' His voice assumed a depth that caused her stomach to execute a slow somersault. 'How was your day?'

'Busy.'

'Very concise.'

'You want detail? Cristo threw a hissy fit when his bechamel sauce curdled and he had to start over. The pan shifted on the gas hob and the flame burnt his finger. It was so not his day.'

'James?'

'I haven't seen him.'

Alessandro hoped it remained that way. Although he doubted Lily's ex-fiancé would give up easily.

'I suggest you be on your guard.'

'I can protect myself, Alessandro.'

Verbally, without doubt. But physically? Sophia's concern for her niece's safety had become his own. Instinct warned he had reason and he'd lived by instinct alone for too many years to consider ignoring it.

'Seven thirty tomorrow evening, Lily,' he reminded quietly.

CHAPTER SEVEN

DECIDING what she should wear to dinner involved a mental selection and discard process throughout the day.

There was a gorgeous jade silk chiffon gown with a fitted bodice and bias cut skirt that skimmed her slim curves, fashioned by a noted Australian designer, which she'd packed to bring to Milan, but had not as yet worn.

A matching wrap added a finishing touch, and with her hair pinned in an upswept style, minimum jewellery, killer heels...decision made.

It wasn't a date, merely the first social engagement without Sophia's presence, Lily assured herself as she put the final touches to her make-up.

She was ready with minutes to spare, and she caught up her evening purse and headed out to the lounge in time to hear the buzz of the in-house phone.

Alessandro. Yet caution had her checking the visual monitor before relaying she was on her way down.

A clutch of nerves rose in her stomach as the lift descended, and she took a deep calming breath scant seconds before the steel doors opened onto the foyer.

This was just dinner. For four, not *à deux*.

So chill, *smile and have a great time.*

Yet she only had to look at him to know she was way out of her depth.

The chiselled facial features, the dark, almost black eyes, which saw much more than she wanted them to. As to his mouth…the memory of how it felt possessing her own was so vivid, she barely controlled a faint quiver.

Deal with it.

And she did, offering a generous smile as she moved to his side. 'Hi.' Too bright, too much?

'*Buona sera*, Liliana.'

There it was again…*Liliana*. Did he know what it did to her?

'Shall we go?'

How was it possible to look forward to sharing dinner with a man who turned her emotions every which way, when all she felt impelled to do was to retreat to safety?

It didn't make sense.

'You're interested in restoring old buildings,' Lily ventured as they purred through the streets. 'Are you working on a project at the moment?'

'Yes. There are various stipulations in place. Permissions to be granted, the submission and approval of plans. The legalities involved. All of which can become a long process.'

'Bureaucracy and red tape while numerous sources confer, consult and compare,' she lightly posed, and glimpsed his wry smile.

'Occasionally for several months.'

'I imagine patience is key.'

He spared her a glance. 'You don't consider me to be a patient man?'

Lily considered him carefully. 'Perhaps,' she conceded. 'If you wanted something enough.'

The man seated at her side was capable of achieving whatever he wanted, by whatever means it took to gain his objective. For beneath the sophisticated exterior was a ruthlessness born from a need to survive at any cost.

A loyal friend, she perceived, but a dangerous adversary.

It didn't help that she was incredibly *aware* of him, the primitive sensuality he generated with no seeming effort at all. He had the *look* of a man who knew everything there was to know about women, what they wanted, *needed,* and the skill to deliver—in bed, and out of it.

Where had that come from?

Like she *needed* another man's touch?

She'd sworn off men, remember? *All* men.

Especially men of Alessandro's calibre. With whom even the lightest dalliance would be akin to treading a precarious path through an emotional minefield.

The light touch of his hand at the back of her waist felt warm, almost protective as he guided her towards the bar where Giarda and Massimo were seated.

Giarda stood and brushed her lips to Lily's cheek. 'It is so good to see you both,' she greeted, and repeated the action with Alessandro, with Massimo following suit.

'We shall have a drink together before moving

to our table,' Giarda indicated, and Massimo's eyes gleamed with latent humour.

'My wife likes to be in charge.'

'Because it amuses you to allow me to do so,' Giarda responded sweetly.

The chemistry between them was almost palpable, and Lily felt a momentary tinge of envy. They looked so *good* together, so *right*. It made her faintly wistful that such a shared passion would be missing from her own life.

Once bitten, twice shy...kind of said it all.

It was interesting to see that both Alessandro and Massimo appeared to be the best of friends, as well as business associates. Any past rivalry had obviously been dispensed with long ago.

The restaurant seemed to be a favourite among the social elite, of whom Massimo, Giarda and Alessandro obviously ranked highly, given the almost obsequious attention accorded them by the maître d' and wait-staff.

The food was perfection, the presentation superb. On a scale of one to ten, Lily mentally afforded top marks.

They had just finished the main course when Giarda lifted her goblet of wine and took an appreciative sip, then returned the goblet to the table.

'In a couple of weeks Massimo and I celebrate our fifth wedding anniversary,' she began, pausing to smile at her husband. 'We are hosting a party at our Lake Maggiore villa on the Saturday evening, and we want to invite you both for the weekend to share the celebration with us. There will be a Sunday brunch on board as we cruise the lakes. It will be wonderful to have you join us,' she concluded with genuine warmth.

'*Grazie*, Giarda,' Alessandro said with an affectionate smile. 'We accept with pleasure.'

Lily's eyes widened. *Hang on a minute, there is no* we. Besides, she was rostered to work on Saturday *and* Sunday for the next few weeks.

'I'm afraid I'll have to decline,' Lily said with regret. 'I'll be working the weekend.'

Giarda looked genuinely disappointed for a few seconds, then she smiled. 'I'm sure if you approach your boss, he will arrange for you to reschedule.'

Saturday evening was usually a restaurant's busiest night. 'I don't think it will be possible.'

'Lily, promise me you will ask,' Giarda pleaded persuasively, and Lily inclined her head.

'I'll approach the head chef tomorrow.'

'You could go straight to the top and ask your boss now.'

To place a call on her cell-phone during dinner seemed incredibly impolite, and she was about to say so when Giarda offered quietly,

'He is seated at this table.'

Lily's eyes widened with surprise as she cast a startled glance at Massimo, who silently indicated Alessandro.

Alessandro owned the restaurant where she worked?

It took mere seconds for everything to click into place. Sophia's choice of restaurant for lunch, the opportunity to work there. Happenstance was a fine thing, but in this instance it seemed *too* coincidental not to have been preplanned.

She cast him a deliberately bright smile before turning towards Giarda. 'In that case, rescheduling my weekend shift won't be a problem.'

'Good. It is settled. We will look forward to seeing you both mid-afternoon.'

'Thank you,' Lily added politely. 'I'll look forward to it.'

Somehow she managed to get through the remainder of the evening, although acting a part while inwardly seething took some effort.

It didn't help when Alessandro placed an arm along the back of her chair as the waitress served them coffee.

A casual gesture, it succeeded in tripping her pulse, not to mention heightening her awareness of him, the refined exclusiveness of his cologne. *Dammit,* everything about him.

Bidding Giarda and Massimo goodnight involved several minutes as they exchanged pleasantries before parting to collect their car.

Lily waited until Alessandro ignited the engine and they joined the flow of traffic.

'How did it go down, Alessandro?' she queried with deceptive lightness. 'And don't insult my intelligence by fudging fact.'

'I wouldn't dream of it.'

She directed him a dark look, which should have felled him, but had no effect at all. 'Sophia could have selected any one of many restaurants to share lunch that day.'

'It concerns you that she chose mine?'

Her eyes flashed in the reflected light of on-coming traffic. 'Only that it reeks of being a deliberate set-up.'

'And that angers you?'

'I dislike being deceived. Or being given an unfair advantage.'

'You earned your employment,' he reminded silkily. 'You're a professional chef, you own and head a restaurant, and you happen to speak fluent French and Italian.'

'Tell me…if I'd walked in off the street as an unknown and asked for employment, would I have succeeded?'

'Probably not.'

Lily's eyes darkened measurably as he eased to a halt outside her apartment building and cut the engine.

It irked unbearably that he had merely been kind due to his connection with Sophia. Doubtless he viewed it as a duty, and probably found her company boring.

'No.'

Lily's eyes flared a little. 'Excuse me?'

'No.' he reiterated quietly as he released his seat belt.

'You have no idea what—'

'You're thinking? Try me.'

He framed her face and lowered his mouth within a hair's breadth of her own. Then his mouth covered her own, seeking, persuasive, his touch skilful as he tasted the inner sweetness, coaxing until a reluctant groan rose unbidden deep in her throat and she gave in to the need to savour his touch, to exult in the mastery he gifted her.

It was more, so much *more* than she'd imagined as she became lost…so involved that she whimpered as he began to ease back.

For what seemed an age he simply looked at her, and the breath hitched raggedly in her throat as he smoothed a gentle thumb over her lower lip.

'Now you understand.'

Did she?

Oh, dear heaven. 'I can't. You…' Her eyes registered stark disbelief, *shock*…at the passion they'd just shared. 'I have to…' She pulled away from him, barely aware that he let her go as she fumbled with the seat belt, then she reached for the door clasp and scrambled out from the car.

Her key...*dammit,* where was her *key?*

'Your purse.'

When had he emerged from behind the wheel and moved to her side?

Somehow she extracted her keys, and she was unaware he moved with her to the main entrance, or that he followed her into the lobby until they reached the lift.

'Please...just go.'

'When I've seen you safely inside your apartment.'

'No,' Lily protested. 'I'm fine.'

Sure you are. Admit it...you're an emotional mess.

The lift door slid open and he followed her in, pressed the appropriate button, and regarded her pensively as the lift travelled to her floor.

Without a word he took the keys from her hand and inserted the right key into the lock and opened the door before handing the bunch back to her. *'Buona notte, cara.* I'll call you tomorrow.'

She shook her head helplessly.

'Lock the door behind me.'

She did so, her actions on autopilot as she crossed to her bedroom to stand staring sightlessly into space, until reality intervened.

With automatic movements she slid off her stilettos, then she discarded her clothes before entering the en suite.

Her fingers trembled as she removed the pins from her hair and swept it into a loose tail. It was then she caught sight of her reflection and closed her eyes to temporarily block out the image—pale face, huge eyes, a swollen well-kissed mouth.

Oh, my.

Where did she go from here?

CHAPTER EIGHT

LILY CHECKED HER ROSTER, noted her next free day, and called Sophia.

Family, she accorded wistfully. True friends were gold, but beloved family represented the finest of precious jewels.

'I have a free day on Wednesday,' Lily explained when they'd exchanged mutual news. 'I'd love to have you to dinner at my place. Carlo, too, of course.' She paused fractionally. 'And Alessandro.'

If Sophia noticed the slight change in Lily's voice, she chose not to comment. 'I accept with pleasure. You will contact Alessandro?'

'Yes.' Doing so was a given, although just *thinking* about making the call had her stomach doing a slow somersault. 'Does seven-thirty suit?'

'Perfect. I'm so looking forward to it.'

'It'll be great,' Lily responded with genuine warmth.

With Sophia and Carlo, *yes.* Alessandro's presence…not so much.

So why do you go to pieces whenever you see him?

Melt when he touches you, even in the most casual manner? And let's not *think* about the way his mouth feels on your own…*lethal,* she admitted.

So make the call, why don't you? Get it over with before you need to leave for the afternoon shift. After all, what could be easier…you have his cell-phone number on speed-dial.

He answered on the second ring. 'Lily. What can I do for you?'

She was tempted to tell him, except that would be most unwise. 'I've invited Sophia and Carlo to dinner on Wednesday evening. Are you free to join us?'

'It will be a pleasure.' His voice held a warm sensuality that sent her pulse-beat into overdrive.

'Seven-thirty, my place.' She got the details out quickly, adding, *'Ciao'* before ending the connection.

There, it was done.

In his luxurious office Alessandro put down the phone and contained a slight smile. He received many invitations over the course of each year, among them social, and the intimate kind. But none, he mused, that had been issued with such polite reluctance.

Lily…or Liliana, as he preferred to think of her, was a piece of work. Warm, charming, delightful, when she let down her guard.

A welcome change from women who played the seductive game for any man sufficiently wealthy to afford the lifestyle they craved. Their bodies sculptured to what they perceived as perfection, their adopted façade so practised they became carbon copies of each other.

He could name a dozen or more he could call who would drop everything to be by his side.

Except Lily Parisi, the one woman he wanted, who kissed like an angel and fitted into his arms as if she was meant to be there.

He intended that she would, eventually. When he'd succeeded in earning her trust.

Time and patience...he possessed both.
And he always won.

The night was busy, with every table filled in the restaurant. Which involved kitchen and wait staff working with maximum efficiency.

Lily was beginning to feel comfortable and part of a valued team. Any reserve on Giovanni's part no longer existed, and Cristo, even at his temperamental best, she could usually succeed in making him smile.

Of the wait-staff, she shared an empathy with Hannah, whose sense of humour and facial expressions on occasion lightened the load. Especially when the occupants of a table chose to place an order and expect a gourmet dish be delivered in a matter of minutes.

Giovanni, who usually held everyone together with unruffled calm, was known to vent *sotto voce*, that he ran a first class restaurant, not a franchised fast-food chain.

As in any restaurant, on occasion, there appeared the guest who felt empowered to impress *loudly* with his knowledge of wine, assuring anyone who cared to listen that he was a noted connoisseur of fine food, only to view the dish he'd ordered with a disappointed sigh, appear to reluctantly fork a sample taste into his mouth, deliberately test the morsel and give a slight but expressive shrug as if to convey it failed to meet his expectation.

Then there was the guest who found fault with everything, and made such a production of sending each dish back to the kitchen, after consuming part of it, in a ploy to gain a complimentary meal.

A good lurk if you could work it, and there were the few who attempted to try.

Lily reached the end of her shift, removed her apron and tossed it into the laundry bin, and was about to leave when Hannah caught her attention.

'We're both on the lunch shift tomorrow. What say we share a coffee together when we're done?'

'Love to.' Lily gave a quick smile and received an impish grin in response.

It would be fun, Lily reflected on the edge of sleep. Hannah was of a similar age and they shared the same interests.

'You choose,' Lily declared as they finished up

the following day. 'You've been in Milan longer than I have.'

'One year and counting,' Hannah agreed. 'There's this little café a few streets away that serves divine coffee.'

'Then let's go.'

It was small but cosy, and they chose a table, ordered a *latte* each, and it was Hannah who spoke first.

'Is this where we exchange our life stories, commiserate or rejoice?' Her eyes gleamed with mischief. 'Or do we forget all that and discuss something meaningful and dull?'

'What if the life story is dull?'

'Impossible. The kitchen goss pegs you as owning your own restaurant, you're Italian by birth, and a professional match for Giovanni and Cristo.'

Lily gave a light laugh and spread her hands. 'Well, there you have it. Your turn.'

'Uh-huh. More details.'

'Not much to tell. My aunt invited me to visit, and I decided to stay a while.'

'Boyfriend break-up?'

'Something like that.'

'Same goes. Relationship growing stale. Thought if I left London, he'd miss me and follow. He didn't.'

Their *lattes* served, they each took an appreciative sip.

'I'm kind of seeing someone,' Hannah confided. 'He's Italian.'

Lily smiled. 'That's nice.'

Hannah rolled her eyes and shook her head. 'His mother wants to see him settle down with an Italian girl, follow tradition and bear him fine sons. Not an English girl who has different ideas and doesn't speak the language.'

'And what does this man you're kind of seeing have to say?'

'It's his life, and he'll choose his own wife.'

'Sounds as if he knows his own mind.'

Hannah's eyes glowed with warmth. 'Yeah. He does.'

'So what's the problem?'

'Italian mothers tend to be very protective of their sons,' she answered drily. *'Famiglia.* I don't fit in.'

'Simple. You keep him happy and win his mother over with your cooking skills.'

'No problem keeping him happy,' Hannah assured with a suggestive wriggle of her eyebrows. 'I can cook. And I've been taking lessons in Italian.'

'Well, then, you have nothing to worry about.'

She brightened a little. 'What about you? Are you seeing anyone?'

Lily laughed. 'Hey, I've only been in Milan a short while.'

'There's a rumour you have connections with Alessandro del Marco, the restaurant's owner.'

Lily kept her voice even. 'He's a friend of my aunt.'

'He dines at the restaurant occasionally. Prime,' Hannah accorded with a wicked grin. 'Bet he's fantastic in bed.'

'I wouldn't know.'

Hannah rolled her eyes in expressive disbelief. 'And don't want to?'

'No.'

'Shame.'

They lingered a while, finished their coffee, then they parted as Hannah headed to the rail station and Lily made her way to her car.

Wednesday she rose early, cleaned the apartment, then she pondered the evening's dinner menu as she ate breakfast.

Linguini with a delicate *funghi* sauce as a starter, she decided, followed by a revered Parisi specialty chicken dish, and a delicate fruit torte as dessert, a mango sorbet to cleanse the palate. Coffee. And wine.

Simple, not too fussy, good wholesome family food. Not a visual work of cuisine art for clientele.

Lily checked her pantry, made a comprehensive list, and shopped for the ingredients needed.

Everything was in place by early evening, the table set, wine chilling, the torte resting in the refrigerator.

Time to dispense with jeans and top, shower, don something feminine, fix her hair, and add a touch of lip gloss.

The in-house phone buzzed at seven-thirty, and when she picked up it was Alessandro's visual image displayed on the video monitor, not Sophia and Carlo as she'd hoped would appear first.

Lily felt her heartbeat quicken its pace as she released the external door allowing entry into the downstairs lobby.

All too soon he reached her apartment, and she let him in with what she hoped was a welcoming smile, accepted the gift bottle of wine, offered her thanks, then her eyes flew wide as he cradled her face and kissed her.

A little too thoroughly, for her peace of mind.

'Nice,' Alessandro murmured appreciatively as he lifted his head to regard her with quizzical warmth.

Nice? Apropos the kiss, *her,* the apartment, the tantalizing aroma of food simmering on stove top and in the oven?

Like she intended to ask?

Fortunately it was only a matter of minutes before the in-house phone buzzed, announcing Sophia and Carlo's arrival.

Did her relief show? She hoped not.

Lily felt the tension ease a little as she assumed the hostess role, offering wine.

'Let me take care of it,' Alessandro said as he moved to her side, and her eyes flared a little as he expertly dispensed with the cork before pouring a portion of wine into each of the four goblets.

With ease he passed them around, then lifted

his goblet and offered a toast. 'Lily. A new and happy life.'

Five minutes, maybe ten, and she'd retreat into the kitchen, set the pasta to cook, transfer the chicken into a serving dish, arrange the vegetables, then as soon as the pasta was ready she'd serve the starter.

There seemed no valid reason for the onset of nerves. She didn't *do* nerves when it came to food. So *why* the feeling she was treading on eggshells? It didn't make sense.

Although, nothing made sense when she happened to be in Alessandro's presence. The air seemed to shimmer with sensual electricity, so much so it almost became a palpable entity.

Was it just her fanciful imagination…or did he sense it, too?

For heaven's sake, she silently chastised. *Get with the programme. Go do what you do best, put the final touches to the starter, retrieve herb bread from the oven, and put food on the table.*

'If you'll excuse me?'

'Would you like some help?' Sophia queried.

'I'm fine, thanks.'

It only took a matter of minutes to drain the

linguini, set it on plates and add the delicate *funghi* sauce. The main course rested in warming dishes, ready to transfer to the table.

Lily took a spot check, set the herb bread into a napkin-lined basket, then she called her guests to be seated.

The linguini was declared *perfecto,* the chicken *ambrosia,* and the fruit torte followed by mango sorbet *excellente.*

It was, even in Lily's critical opinion, a satisfactory dinner. Even if she'd been dogged by more nerves than she could remember. A fact she laid solidly at Alessandro's feet.

'Miei complimenti,' Carlo added quietly.

'Grazie,' she accepted with a warm smile, and almost froze as Alessandro brushed light fingers to her cheek.

'Superb, Lily.'

Her eyes dilated, and for a moment she lost the power of speech. 'Thank you,' she managed at last. 'Would you like to move into the lounge while I clear the table? Then we can relax in comfort.'

'It's pleasant to sit around the table for a while, don't you think?' Sophia said wistfully. 'It reminds me of my family, when we caught up with each other, laughed a little and talked a lot.'

'The table it is,' Lily agreed gently. For, like her aunt, she associated food with family camaraderie, for it had been the one time of the day when they were all together...the closeness mattered, and the love.

Any further wine was declined as both men had to drive, and coffee was delayed as they sat informally at the table and exchanged anecdotes.

'Do you remember, Lily,' Sophia began, 'when you visited with your parents? You were, I think, fourteen, or was it fifteen years old?'

Lily chuckled. 'Please don't. I had braces, wore my hair in a tail, I lived in jeans and bewailed the fact I would never be tall.'

'I recall your mother endeavouring to persuade you to wear a dress.'

'While I thought jeans made my legs seem longer, and therefore added the illusion of height.'

'A cute teenager,' Alessandro drawled, sparing her a gleaming look.

Cute? That was what he remembered? Better that, than the way she'd secretly fantasized, no, tell it how it was...*drooled* over the tall handsome young man with a wicked past, whose image invaded her dreams far too often.

Except that was more than ten years ago, and there had been a lot of changes in her life, some good, as she recalled time with her parents, her travels, success as a chef. And more recently, the not so good.

Lily turned towards Alessandro. 'And what of your teenage years, Alessandro?'

His eyes held her own, dark obsidian and bearing an edge of mockery. 'I'm sure you've heard how Giuseppe and Sophia took me into their home, their lives, and shaped me into the man I've become.'

'Yes,' she said quietly. 'I have. But very little of your life before then.'

'It's something I share with very few people.'

'That bad?'

Living hand to mouth, with no home to go to; learning to fight dirty in order to survive on the streets; being one step ahead of the *polizia,* constantly watching his back.

'*Sì.'*

He bore the scars from the slashes he'd taken from knives; tattoos now removed by laser, and the few he'd kept as a reminder of a life he'd left long behind him.

'I'll make coffee,' Lily ventured. 'It's becoming late, and Carlo and Sophia need to return to Como.'

It was a simple matter to grind the coffee beans and set up the coffee machine. She set out the requisite crockery on a tray while she waited for the machine to percolate. Then when it was done, she added the sugar bowl and took it to the table.

Soon Sophia, Carlo and Alessandro would leave, then she'd clean up and retire for the night.

Except it didn't play out that way.

Alessandro stood at her side as Sophia bade them both an affectionate *buona notte* and preceded Carlo from the apartment.

'I thought you might be leaving, too,' Lily said as he closed the door and turned to face her.

'When I've helped you clean up.' He removed his jacket, deftly rolled back his shirtsleeves and moved towards the kitchen.

'It's not necessary.' Her protest went unheeded, and she had little option but to follow him. 'You don't have to do this.'

Be honest, she didn't want him there, invading her space, dominating the room. Worse, she *definitely* didn't want to feel on edge and so acutely aware of him.

'I'll rinse, you stack the dishwasher,' Alessandro said calmly, and proceeded to do just that.

'This happens to be my kitchen…'

'And you'd prefer I wasn't in it,' he said calmly, shooting her a perceptive look. 'Let me know when you've worked out the reason why.'

With deliberate calm she took the rinsed goblets, the plates and cutlery and stacked them carefully. Clattering them noisily would only give him the satisfaction of knowing he'd ruffled her feathers.

When he was done he dried his hands and turned towards her, and she became trapped by the darkness in his eyes, the hint of something she didn't want to explore as he lifted a hand and trailed light fingers down her cheek.

Her eyes flared momentarily before she attempted to mask them, and his own darkened as he cupped her face and touched his mouth to her own, tracing the seam of her lips with the tip of his tongue.

He felt her stiffen, but didn't stop, teasing gently

as he sought her response, which she fought against giving, until her body betrayed her and she succumbed with a despairing groan.

It was a kiss like no other she'd experienced, and she recalled beating a helpless fist against his shoulder as he deepened the kiss into something more before gently releasing her, his hands holding her steady as she stood locked into immobility, wide-eyed with a mixture of shock, dismay and wonder, that she'd allowed him so close.

'I think you should leave,' Lily managed shakily, her eyes darkening as he brushed gentle fingers over the swollen curve of her lower lip.

'If that's what you want.'

Want? She daredn't even consider what she wanted, because if she listened to the heat of desire, she'd lead him into the bedroom, tear off his clothes, her own, and indulge in wild wanton sex.

Except treading that path would only lead to disaster.

He watched as she reassembled her resolve… the way she swallowed a sudden lump in her throat; the telltale pulse slow its rapid beat; the tinge of pink colouring her cheeks.

'Yes.'

He used his thumbs to soothe the curve of her shoulders, then slowly slid his hands down her arms before releasing her.

'Your call.'

His very presence was a threat to her peace of mind, and she crossed her arms over her midriff in a gesture of self-protection. 'I'd prefer not to see you again.'

No sooner were the words out of her mouth before she realized the futility of them. Alessandro del Marco was as much Sophia's son as if he bore the dalla Silvestri name.

He looked at her in silence for what seemed an age, and she had to consciously force herself to meet and hold his gaze.

'Afraid, Lily?'

'Of you? No.' *Myself,* she owned silently, and for a moment she thought she caught a glimpse of humour in his dark gaze as he ventured softly,

'You're sure about that?'

She didn't answer, couldn't for a few heart-stopping seconds. 'Yes.'

'And you'd prefer me to leave.'

'Please.'

He reached for his jacket and shrugged it on as she crossed the lounge to the front door.

'*Grazie*, Lily. For a pleasant evening.'

He made no attempt to touch her, and she tamped down the contrary urge to feel his lips brush her own.

Which was crazy.

'You're welcome.' The polite words were an automatic acknowledgment as she opened the door and stood aside for him to pass.

Then he was gone, and she locked up the apartment, doused the lights and went to bed.

CHAPTER NINE

CRISTO'S absence during the lunch shift meant Lily and Giovanni were required to share the work of three, and, although the kitchen staff co-ordinated as a team, there was the added pressure of ensuring there were minimum delays in plating up and serving orders.

Hectic didn't cover it, and together they breathed a sigh of relief as the lunch shift drew towards an end.

'We made it,' Lily declared as she shared a high-five gesture with Giovanni. 'Amy did well.'

'*Sì,*' he agreed. 'Go take a break for an hour.'

'Thanks.'

Some fresh air and a change of scene would be good, and she removed her apron, head cap, then she collected her shoulder bag and exited the restaurant.

Yoghurt, fruit and a salad roll, juice, and she

collected a daily newspaper as she headed towards a small café where she made her purchases, selected a table, and settled in to skim through the daily news.

She flipped the top of her juice and took an appreciate sip, then unwrapped the salad roll.

'Lily. Mind if I share?'

James? What was he doing here? 'I have nothing to say to you.' Civil, she could do *civil,* in spite of an initial reaction to pick up her food and leave.

He slid into a chair opposite and attempted to take hold of her hand, only to sigh as she instantly removed it out of his reach.

'Can't we at least try to resolve our break-up?'

She met his gaze squarely. 'It is resolved. As in *finito,* finished, over. With not a hope in hell of reconciliation.'

He leant forward in an earnest attempt to redeem himself. 'We shared a great life in Sydney. Surely you can accept I've—'

'Realized the error of your ways, James?'

'Yes. I swear.'

'No.'

His expression hardened. 'That's your final word?'

'Yes. Absolutely. Beyond doubt,' Lily added with emphasis, in the hope he would finally *get* it.

He sat back in his chair. 'Then you leave me no choice.'

She measured him carefully. 'The only sensible choice you could make is to return to Australia.'

'You're going to *pay,* big time,' he vowed with ill-disguised vengeance. 'I've prepared a comprehensive list, waiting to be emailed to my lawyer to file suit to sue.'

'Which no lawyer will touch, given you lived in my home, for which you failed to contribute so much as a cent.'

'There's breach of promise, loss of future benefits, expenses incurred, to name a few. I'm entitled to half your income for the time we were together, the loss of a home in which I expected to reside as your husband. Not to mention a comparable sum to compensate for my grief and heartache resulting in my inability to continue working.'

He really imagined he would succeed? When she had proof to negate any claim he made?

'A cool two million should do it.'

He was out of his mind.

Don't lose it, she bade silently. Anger on her part would only feed the fire.

Lily looked at James, the man she had once thought she loved and planned to marry, and wondered how she could have made such an error in judgment—been so *wrong*.

All along James had wanted her for what she had. A person with whom he could share a cruisy life, and enjoy sexual satiation outside the sanctity of his marriage.

What she'd thought was affection and love was merely an image she'd conjured that had little basis in reality. He'd played a part she'd believed to be genuine…and it hadn't been. Their marriage, if she'd gone ahead with it, wouldn't have lasted long. His *indiscretions* would eventually have come to light, and she'd have filed for divorce.

With enforced calm she stood, collected her shoulder bag, and fastened his truculent gaze with her own. 'Good luck with that. Be aware I'll counter sue,' she added with deadly resolve.

If there was going to be a legal battle, then she'd need to be prepared. An email to her lawyer outlining James's threatened intention would clarify legal right under Australian law.

The dinner shift was even more hectic, if that were possible, than lunch had been, and there was a sense of relief to finish up at evening's end and drive home.

The apartment was silent, and she reset the security system, tossed her keys onto the table, followed them with her shoulder bag, and headed for the shower.

It was late, it had been a long day, and bed had rarely seemed more welcome. Yet she took her time, letting the hot water ease tired muscles before drying off and donning sleepwear.

Then she retrieved her laptop, logged on, checked emails, composed one to her lawyer, and pressed 'Send'. With the differing time zones, he'd receive it during Sydney business hours and she'd have a response within twenty-four hours.

Surprisingly she slept well, and woke feeling refreshed. Perhaps it was because it was her day off, the knowledge James, now he'd shown his hand, would leave Milan, especially *her*, and life would return to normal.

A spur-of-the-moment decision to do some exploring on her own added enthusiasm to the day, and with the aid of a map she sorted out a picturesque route, ate a hasty breakfast, then she caught up her keys and took the lift down to the lobby.

It was cool…OK, cold, although the sky looked clear as she slid in behind the wheel of her car and began heading south west.

There was a yen to wander the Piazza della Vetra linking San Lorenzo to Sant'Eustorgio. She recalled her mother relaying historic events linked to the area, the beautiful churches, and she had the day, the time, and there was a sense of freedom in having no set plan, other than to return to her apartment by sunset.

Music emitted from a disc she slotted into the player, upbeat and mood-elevating, and she smiled, really *smiled* for the first time in a while.

There was a small trattoria where she pulled over and ordered lunch, lingered over a *latte,* then just as she was about to leave the insistent peal of her cell-phone caught her attention.

Alessandro appeared on caller ID, and she picked up. 'Hi.'

She sounded happy, and he leaned back in his chair as he idly viewed the city skyscape. The terracotta roof tiles of aged buildings, the church domes, spires, and the gathering of clouds looming low.

He liked the sound of her voice, the light Australian intonation and lilt apparent. Yet she spoke Italian like a native.

'I have tickets for tonight's performance at the *Teatro alla Scala.*' He named a time. 'I'll collect you.'

'I haven't said I'll accept the invitation.'

'Are you going to refuse?'

La Scala? Are you joking? 'La Scala* is very appealing.'

'Consequently you'll suffer my company in order to enjoy opera,' he drawled with a hint of humour, and heard her soft laughter.

'Yes. But it'll be a stretch.'

'Such a gracious acceptance, Liliana.'

'What would you have me say?' It was easy to

tease, easy to assume a slightly breathless tone.
'*Caro mio, grazie*. I can't wait to see you?'

'That's an improvement.'

'Enjoy it while you can. *Ciao*.'

La Scala, she mused as she paid for her meal.
Dress-up time. Thanks to her shopping expeditions with Sophia, she possessed a choice of
suitable gowns to wear.

She adored opera, and bit back an oath that she
hadn't thought to ask which performance was
scheduled.

Did it matter? Not in the least, and as she set
the car in motion she punched up the volume a
fraction, and sang in tune with the vocalist as the
final track played out.

The day's light was beginning to dim as she
reached her apartment, and she made straight for
the shower, shampooed and dried her hair, she
donned a robe, checked the time, then padded out
to the kitchen to cut up some fresh fruit to eat.

Alessandro hadn't mentioned dinner, which
indicated they'd probably go on somewhere afterwards.

Sophistication *worked* for any occasion, and
Lily tended to her make-up, using a light touch

with emphasis on her eyes and a red lip gloss. The gown in brilliant red complemented her fine textured skin, and she chose to leave her hair loose in a cascade of natural waves that fell just beneath her shoulders. A heart-shaped diamond pendant and matching ear-studs, together with a slim diamond bracelet completed her jewellery, and with minutes to spare she slid her feet into black killer heels, caught up a matching evening purse, keys, a slender wallet containing sufficient euros should she need them, and collected a black coat as the in-house phone rang.

She picked up, saw Alessandro's features, and said, 'On my way down.'

Attired in a black evening suit, white shirt and black bow tie, he projected an enviable aura of power. Strong masculine sculpted features with faint grooves slashing his cheeks, dark almost black eyes, a sensuously shaped mouth... *dynamite.*

'Bella,' he complimented gently as he cupped her shoulders and bestowed a fleeting kiss to her cheek.

'Thank you,' Lily acknowledged, and felt the familiar tightening deep inside at his smile. 'I'm flattered I won out over the numerous names you have in your little black book.'

Alessandro curved an arm around her waist. 'Remind me some time to tell you why.'

His subtle cologne teased her senses as he ushered her to the waiting car and saw her seated before he slipped in behind the wheel.

Traffic was heavy, and it took time to park and enter the Piazza della Scala and join the evening patrons seeking what many would consider to be the ultimate opera experience.

It was impossible not to feel a sense of awe, knowing how long the venue had stood, its history, the famous composers whose works had been sung by equally famous sopranos, contraltos and baritones over time. The costumes, the background scenery. The drama, the voices as the characters' stories were revealed to the accompaniment of glorious music.

Beautiful, enthralling, exquisite…were the descriptive words that came to mind, and she said so during a break between acts.

For the duration, she had forgotten it was Alessandro who sat at her side, for in truth she lost sight of everything except what was happening on stage.

'You are enjoying the evening.'

It was a statement, not a query, and her eyes shone with pleasure as she met his own. 'How could I not?' she answered simply.

He caught hold of her hand and threaded her fingers through his own. *'Bene.'*

Lily told herself the holding hands thing was just a friendly gesture, and tried to deny it felt… nice. A hint of strength in the warmth of his clasp, a sense of protectiveness, and for a while she made no attempt to disengage her hand. Only to have his fingers tighten a little when she did.

There was a sense of disappointment when the final act reached its conclusion and the lights came on, the inevitable crush of people as they lined up at the exits, and eventually the cool evening air as they reached the *piazza.*

'There is a pleasant restaurant not far from here,' Alessandro indicated the direction. 'Are you hungry?'

'Yes,' Lily said at once. 'Ravenous.'

His husky laughter curled round her nerve-ends and tugged a little. 'Then we shall eat.'

There was a sense of intimacy in the way his arm curved along the back of her waist, and she wanted to deny that she liked the feel of it resting there a little too much.

Even in stiletto heels, her eyes were barely level with his black bow tie, and if she were to lean in against him, her head would fit into the curve of his shoulder.

Just for an instant she was strongly tempted to move closer, except that would provide a message she wasn't ready to deliver.

The restaurant Alessandro chose was well patronized, and the greeting he received from the maître d' was little less than obsequious as they were led to a quiet curved booth in one corner.

'Bottled water, Pellegrino,' Lily indicated when Alessandro suggested wine, and she ordered an entrée of risotto with sautéed mushrooms sprinkled with fresh parsley.

A light meal perfect for this late hour, although Alessandro selected a main course, and waived the wine.

There was a sense of…what? Friendship? More than that, Lily admitted. *More* than mere duty to the niece of a woman he held in such high regard.

Slowly, steadily, he was invading her mind, stirring emotions she'd prefer were left dormant.

Yet there was something elusive simmering between them, a sense of inevitability…almost as if she were being gently led along a preordained path.

Leading *where*?

She didn't want to be caught up, body and soul. *His,* irrevocably, but for how long? A few weeks, months maybe? Then what? A gentle distancing? A return to mere friendship? Acknowledging him on social occasions. Worse, so much worse would be seeing him with another woman and feeling totally torn apart.

'You're thinking too much.'

Lily lifted solemn eyes to meet his own, and offered, 'It's a female thing.'

'Questions,' he posed quietly, 'to which you seek answers?'

He was far too perceptive, and she wasn't comfortable with it. 'I already know the answers.'

'I'm sure you imagine you do.'

There was an inference apparent she was reluctant to explore.

'It's been a lovely evening. Thank you for inviting me to join you.'

'You're welcome.' With that he signalled the waiter, paid the bill, adding a generous tip, and cast her a musing look. 'Shall we leave?'

They walked to where he'd parked the car, and as soon as they became mobile he activated the CD player.

Verdi emitted from the speakers, and Lily leant back against the headrest and closed her eyes, lost to the music and a host of powerful images.

It was almost a disappointment when the car drew to a halt outside her apartment.

Alessandro released his seat belt, then her own and reached for her, ceasing whatever she had been about to say with the simple expediency of covering her mouth with his own.

No words, just action, as he teased and tasted the sweetness within, encouraging her response until she wound her arms around his neck and held on. Only to still as his hand slid to cup her breast.

The soft brush of his thumb over the sensitive peak brought a faint groan low in her throat as sensation arrowed deep inside.

For a moment she remained immobile, then sanity prevailed and she struggled to be free of him. Surprise and relief meshing together as he slowly eased back.

His eyes were almost black, their expression impossible to define as she instinctively used the flat of her hands against his chest to effect some leverage.

'I...must go.' *Dear heaven.* She collected her evening purse and reached blindly for the door-clasp. 'Thanks,' she managed as she opened the door and slid out as Alessandro offered,

'*Dormire bene.*'

Sleep well.

As if she could manage that easily after losing herself in the intoxicating magic he managed to bestow. Without a word she carefully closed the car door, then she walked, when she was tempted to run, to the entrance, punched in the security code, and moved into the lobby the instant the external door released.

It was just a kiss, she assured as she rode the lift to the third floor.

A very *good* kiss, Lily reflected when she was safely ensconced in her apartment.

OK, *amazing*, she admitted as she lay awake coveting sleep.

What would it be like to…?

Don't even go there.

It's not going to happen.

'What is it with this guy on table five?'

Lily looked up from plating an order and met Hannah's exasperated expression. 'Something wrong?'

'He's sent back his starter with a complaint about the prawns. Says they're overcooked.'

Giovanni had prepared the prawns himself, and they were perfect. 'I'll plate up another starter.' And she deftly did so, placing it ready for Hannah to serve.

Back it came, and this time Hannah rolled her eyes. 'A touch too much dressing on the salad.'

Lily cast a disbelieving glance. 'You have to be joking?'

'Uh-huh. He has something going on, I swear.'

'OK. This time serve the dressing separately so he can add it himself.'

Five minutes later Hannah returned and lifted

her thumb in a positive gesture as she collected another order.

Hallelujah.

Lily really shouldn't have celebrated quite so soon, and the *fussy* customer, as he was now referred to, returned his second course, this time with the complaint there was an abundance of sauce on the *fettuccini.*

Lily bit back an expressive oath, and set up another plate. Only to have it returned minutes later with the words, 'Not enough sauce.'

A fresh plate went out, this time with the sauce in a separate bowl.

Hannah returned it with a thunderous expression, and Lily threw up her hands with a strongly muttered 'What now?'

'Tomato base a fraction too acidic.' Hannah executed an expressive eye-roll.

Given it was Giovanni's much-lauded recipe which *no one* ever faulted, it was obvious the customer was no longer picky, but out to cause trouble.

'If you thought things couldn't get worse... think again. Alessandro del Marco has just entered the restaurant.'

'To dine?'

'He's talking with Giorgio.'

Why did she get the feeling the rest of the evening was going to take a downward spiral?

'Request the guy at table five makes a different selection.'

Hannah breathed in deeply, then exhaled. 'I'll suggest the marinara. If he objects to *that,* I may accidentally on purpose ensure the contents of the plate end up on his lap.'

'Oh, please,' Lily vented very quietly. 'Allow me the pleasure.'

Minutes later Hannah returned. 'He'll accept *fettuccini marinara.*'

Lily shot her a look that indicated more than mere words could convey. 'Will he, indeed?' She set it up, and spooned the portion of *marinara* sauce into a bowl. 'Return that to Mr Fussy, with the chef's compliments. And smile nicely.'

'If I *must.*' Hannah offered a questionable gesture. 'OK, play nice. Got it.'

Lily did her best not to laugh as Hannah sailed out of the kitchen.

Faux humour that soon died when Hannah returned with the plate and bowl in hand. 'I swear...' Lily trailed with barely suppressed anger.

'Hold it, sweetie. He wants to see the chef.'

Lily straightened. 'Does he now?' She took a fresh plate, added pasta, *marinara* sauce, and tilted her head.

'You're not going to...' Hannah began in hushed disbelief as Lily began walking towards the kitchen door.

Lily looked back over one shoulder. 'Watch me. Table five, you said?'

Smile, she bade silently. *Play nice.*

And she did, she even chanced a quick glance towards the table Alessandro occupied, until she saw precisely *who* occupied table five.

James.

Playing nice went out of the window, or door, in this instance.

'*Buona sera,*' Lily offered with such chilling politeness it was a wonder the contents of his glass didn't instantly freeze. 'I understand you have a complaint about your meal.'

He directed her a superior look. 'Yes. I returned the starter *several* times, and I'm not at all happy with the *fettuccini.*'

'I understand, sir. The waitress has relayed your comments.' She extended the plate with its perfectly presented pasta. 'A fresh batch of *marinara* sauce has been especially prepared for you. With the compliments of the management.' She placed the plate onto the table just a little too close to the edge, and as she removed her hand her fingers *accidentally* tilted the plate's rim, causing the contents to slide onto his lap.

'Oh, my goodness,' Lily exclaimed with feigned distress. 'I am *so* sorry.' She whipped a spare napkin from the table and collected a spoon. 'Please, let me clean this up.'

'Get away from me!' James roared, and cursed beneath his breath.

'My sincere apologies,' she offered politely. 'Maître d'!'

Giorgio, the sweetheart, took the situation in at a glance, and immediately expressed his concern. 'An unfortunate accident, sir. You will, of course, be compensated for the dry-cleaning.'

'It was deliberate. She deserves to be fired!'

'I suggest you leave,' a familiar voice drawled with dangerous calm, and Lily watched James's features pale as he recognized *who* stood before him.

'You!' He began to bluster… 'What the hell are you doing here?'

Alessandro arched an expressive eyebrow. 'You have the choice of leaving quietly of your own free will, or being forcibly ejected. You have one minute to choose.'

'You have no right—'

Alessandro's expression hardened into an iron-like mask. 'You're upsetting the clientele in a restaurant I own. You want me to call the police and have them charge you? Twenty-five seconds…'

James didn't move.

Lily unconsciously held her breath as the seconds counted down.

As they reached *zero,* Alessandro spun James round, caught hold of both his hands, and forcibly marched James from the restaurant.

It was over before it really began, and with a quiet word from Giorgio Lily and Hannah returned to the kitchen.

'In a word…wow,' Hannah voiced with a degree of awe.

And then, some, Lily added silently as she checked the next order and began plating up.

Five minutes later the kitchen door swung open and Alessandro entered the kitchen and crossed to Lily's side.

'Your shift is over…as of now.'

She looked at him carefully. 'No, it's not.'

'I say it is.' He reached for the ties at her waist and released them, then he removed the cap from her hair. 'Let's go.'

'I have an obligation—'

'One I've dispensed with.'

'Are you firing me?'

'No.'

Well, then. At least she was still employed. 'I'll collect my bag.'

'We'll take my car,' Alessandro indicated as they emerged from the restaurant. 'I doubt you've eaten, and neither have I.'

Traffic was constant at this time of night, and Lily didn't take particular note of their direction until he slid to a halt outside his apartment building.

'Why have you brought me here?'

'You'd prefer a restaurant filled with people?'

Not really.

'We'll fix a meal, share a glass of wine...'

'And then you'll take me home.'

'If that's what you want.'

'Yes,' she said simply.

There was a sense of camaraderie as they shared the kitchen. Lily took eggs, cheese, tomatoes, herbs and whipped up two savoury omelettes while Alessandro prepared a salad.

Simple fare, which they ate at the kitchen table, together with crunchy bread rolls and a glass of white wine.

He'd discarded his jacket, removed his tie, loosened the top buttons on his shirt and turned back the sleeves.

He was something else, she mused. Relaxed and vastly different from the man who'd called James's bluff and orchestrated a forcible ejection more than an hour ago.

'I don't see any grazes or bruises,' she offered lightly as she met his quizzical expression.

'I no longer need to use my fists to enforce a point.'

'I'm sure there were occasions when you didn't have any choice.'

'It's an old story.'

'And one you don't want to share with me.'

Alessandro sank back in his chair. 'They were years I'm not particularly proud of.'

'You survived,' Lily said quietly.

'By questionable means.'

'Were you responsible for killing anyone?'

'Not by my own hand.' He'd witnessed two of his friends bleed out before an ambulance arrived too late to save either one of them.

'How old were you?'

'Ten and a half years.' The *half* meant something back then.

'You were with foster parents?'

'The third lot. There were others. At age thirteen I chose to fend for myself. On the streets, living hand to mouth, bedding down wherever I could.'

'What age were you when Giuseppe and Sophia took you into their home?'

'Fifteen, almost sixteen.'

'And the years between thirteen and almost sixteen?'

'Curiosity, Lily?'

'Interest,' she corrected, holding his gaze.

'I had a knack with electronics. Gadgets, computers, I could fix them, and it began to pay off.'

'And somehow you caught Giuseppe's notice.'

'Yes.'

Her heart ached for the boy he'd been. Aware the bare facts he'd relayed were only the tip of the iceberg.

Nothing of the fear that must have been his constant companion. The need to be fleet of foot and hand; to be able to fight hard to protect himself and what few belongings he owned.

No child deserved that.

'I doubt you want my sympathy,' she ventured at last. 'So I won't offer it. Instead, I'll say how much I admire you for turning your life around and succeeding against incredible odds.'

There were emotions too close to the surface, and she needed a distraction to control them.

'Dishes,' she announced as she got to her feet. 'Then you get to take me home.'

'Leave them.'

Lily collected plates, flatware and carried them to the counter, rinsed and stacked the dishwasher, then she dealt with the skillet. 'Done.'

She turned to face him, and saw that he stood close by.

'You could stay.'

No, she really couldn't. 'Please don't ask that of me.'

She dried her hands and crossed to where she'd left her bag. 'I'll call a taxi.'

'A taxi isn't an option,' Alessandro said as he collected his keys.

There wasn't a thing she could think of to say as they purred through the streets in Alessandro's car, and she reached for the door-clasp the instant he brought the car to a halt adjacent her apartment building.

'Thanks.'

'I'll see you safely indoors.'

'I'll be fine.'

But Lily knew her emotions were too close to the surface, haunted by images of the lost child he'd been and what he must have suffered.

The lobby was empty, and she crossed to the lift, inserted her key and prayed for it to arrive before tears threatened to spill down her cheeks.

'You don't need to come up with me.'

He didn't say a word as he followed her in,

pressed the designated button for her floor and emerged with her when the lift slid to a halt.

'Give me your keys.'

He took them from her hand and unlocked the door.

Lily blinked rapidly as one tear broke free and rolled slowly down to rest at the corner of her mouth.

Any hope it would go unnoticed was lost as Alessandro closed the door behind them and tilted her face.

'Tears, Liliana?'

'An eyelash in my eye.'

'Of course,' he said gently as he dispensed the traitorous rivulet with his thumb before lowering his head to capture her mouth with his own.

A light sensual caress that soothed as he cradled her face, then he released her and trailed light fingers down her cheek.

'I'll call you.'

CHAPTER TEN

LILY worked a double shift Thursday, and retired to bed utterly beat, for it had been one of *those* when anything that could go wrong, *did*...from an apprentice breaking down in tears when Cristo lost his cool with the poor girl after demanding she quicken her pace or she'd never make chef.

Giovanni, to give him credit, had defused the situation and assigned Lily to oversee.

A love of food was a necessity; knowing the ingredients all-important; creative passion ranked right up there.

Working a professional kitchen involved *knowing* what was required and achieving it with deft accuracy in a *timely manner*. Something that could only be acquired with practice.

Lily could vividly recall sessions wielding a knife to slice and dice beneath her parents' eagle eye in the Parisi kitchen.

'I don't think I can work with him,' the girl declared quietly. 'He's a temperamental monster.'

'Cristo is a perfectionist,' Lily corrected. 'He takes pride in his work, and he demands the same degree of perfection from everyone else.'

'I didn't think it would be this *hard*.'

'Do you *want* to be a chef?'

'More than anything else in the world.'

'Then stiffen up,' Lily offered gently. 'Show Cristo what you're made of, and earn his approval.'

'Does he ever *approve* anything?'

Lily's eyes lit with humour. 'Occasionally.'

Yet there had been further incidents, one in particular where Lily quietly berated Cristo in his native tongue.

A long and fraught day, she concluded wryly as she disposed of her apron, collected her bag and exited the restaurant and walked to where her car was parked.

Friday didn't appear to fare much better, for within minutes of entering the restaurant it became apparent Cristo's taskmaster skills had moved up a few notches, and any camaraderie in the kitchen went out the window...until Amy, the

apprentice chef, inadvertently succeeded in toss-
ing the contents of a pan a little too vigorously,
which resulted in the contents spilling onto the
gas hob and sent the pan clattering to the floor.
Worse, her effort to catch the pan caused the
naked flame to sear her hand.

Fellow staff paused in what they were doing,
and Lily, who was closest, swiftly reached for a
towel, only to have it taken out of her hand by
Cristo.

Within a matter of seconds he doused it with
cold water and gently wrapped it over Amy's
hand.

'It hurts, *sì*?'

'I'm sorry.' Two tears rolled down her cheeks,
and Lily watched, as indeed the others did, as
Cristo merely placed a hand on Amy's shoulder.

'It is nothing. An accident,' he dismissed quietly. 'Can you continue?'

'Yes.'

A slight smile lifted the corners of his mouth.
'Break for five minutes.'

With that he returned to his station and it was
as if the incident hadn't happened.

Well, Lily breathed, so there was a soft heart beneath the temperamental exterior after all.

The restaurant was fully booked for the evening, and everything moved up a pace as the kitchen staff coped with plating orders on time.

It was late when Lily exited the restaurant, and once home she stripped off her clothes and indulged in a leisurely shower, then dry she donned sleep-wear, caught up her laptop and slid into bed to check the daily email from Parisi before closing down in an effort to sleep.

Difficult, given her mind inevitably strayed to Giarda and Massimo's party and her increasing concern Giarda had assumed Lily and Alessandro were a couple and accommodated them in the same suite.

Surely Alessandro would correct that?

But what if he didn't?

Lily was ready with her bag packed when the in-house phone rang at three. She checked the video screen, relayed she was on her way down, and emerged into the foyer to see Alessandro standing a few metres distant.

The impeccable business suit and tie were absent. In their place were casual chinos, a dark navy polo knit shirt that hugged his muscular shoulders, and sunglasses propped on top of his head.

'Hi.' She offered a bright smile as she handed over her bag, only to feel her eyes widen as he leant forward and brushed his lips to her cheek.

He placed an arm loosely along the back of her waist. 'Shall we leave?'

The black sports car was parked out front, and he unlocked the passenger door, saw her seated, then he crossed round the back and stowed her bag in the trunk before slipping in behind the wheel.

Lily waited until they were heading north on the A8 autostrada before broaching the somewhat delicate matter of weekend accommodation… specifically *theirs*.

She met Alessandro's brief studied glance before he returned his attention to the motorway.

'Afraid, Lily?'

'Of you—no.'

'Don't presume to judge me by the actions of other men.'

She closed her eyes, then opened them again,

grateful for the tinted lens of her sunglasses. 'That wasn't my intention.'

'I'm relieved to hear it.'

She was the one with the problem, for it was she who had responded to his kiss—if you could call such a provocatively sensual joining of mouths a kiss—with such fervour as to lead him to think she was willing to allow the passionate exchange to progress into something *more*.

It didn't help *knowing* with instinctive certainty she'd never emerge from a liaison with Alessandro with her emotions intact.

So don't go there.

'Relax, Lily.'

Like she could do that?

Giarda's home was reached via a winding road high on a hillside overlooking Lake Maggiore. A beautiful two-storied villa set among spacious landscaped grounds whose entry was guarded by high ornately designed steel gates, which automatically swung open as they approached.

Giarda and Massimo emerged as Alessandro brought the car to a halt adjacent the main entrance.

Giarda greeted them with affection, tucking

her arm through Lily's own as she led the way indoors. 'It is so good to see you.'

A large marble-tiled foyer showcased a curved double staircase leading to the upper level. Original art graced the walls, and sun streamed through French doors.

'Come, we will take you upstairs to your suite.'

Suite...as in one?

Perhaps she misheard, Lily decided as they reached the atrium at the head of the stairs.

'I have put you in the guest wing. I am sure you will be very comfortable.' Giarda indicated a door at the end of the hallway. 'Here it is quite private, and you have a beautiful view over the lake.'

The view was inspiring, the room large with an adjoining en suite.

One suite...with *two* queen-size beds.

'Thank you,' Lily managed. 'It's perfect.'

'I knew you would like it.'

What was not to like? Lovely furniture and fittings, elegant drapes, an exquisite escritoire, and a marble en suite to die for.

'Settle in, unpack, relax a little. Then you must join us...shall we say, half an hour?'

Giarda preceded Massimo from the room, and Lily turned towards Alessandro the instant the door closed.

'Which bed do you want?'

A slight smile lifted the edges of his mouth. 'You don't wish to share?'

She met his intent gaze, and held it. 'No.'

'Shame.'

He was amused, damn him. His eyes gleamed as he gave a husky chuckle as he lifted his bag onto the nearest bed and freed the zip fastener. 'Any preference for left or right side of the ward-robe?'

Given it was a sizable walk-in, she merely lifted a hand in a careless gesture. 'Be my guest.'

The evening lay ahead, there would be com-pany, and in the evening the party would last well past midnight. By which time they would retire here and inevitably fall asleep within minutes.

Tomorrow there would be a late brunch on board as they cruised the lake, and they would head home before dark.

It was remarkably simple. She had absolutely nothing to worry about.

Except Lily hadn't factored in changing clothes as the time approached to dress for the party.

It irked that Alessandro didn't seem to give a thought to shedding casual wear for a formal evening suit, while she had no intention of stripping down to bra and briefs in his presence.

Instead she gathered the red evening gown she'd purchased in Sophia's company, the red matching set of lingerie, and swept into the en suite without sparing a glance in his direction.

Only to emerge half an hour later, hair and make-up perfect.

'Beautiful.'

She executed a mock curtsy. 'I'm glad you approve.'

It seemed a precaution to tuck her arm through his as they descended the staircase. Killer heels and stairs did not make a good combination when it came to safety.

The party was in full swing as they entered what had to be the ballroom, and at a guess there were upwards of seventy guests mingling as they sipped champagne from crystal flutes, while availing themselves from an abundance of finger food offered by several uniformed waiters.

Muted music made it possible to converse, and Lily recognized a few of the guests, made polite and greeted them, exchanged small talk, and determined to enjoy herself.

Which she did, as Giarda and Massimo had provided entertainment, and there was a DJ spinning discs for those who wanted to be active and dance.

'Alessandro darling. I was sure you'd be here tonight.'

A vision of loveliness with, Lily deduced, a yen for Botox. No one possessed a forehead so incredibly smooth.

Which was hardly fair, given it was every woman's prerogative to look their best.

'Chantelle.' His greeting was sufficiently warm for Lily to wonder at their connection.

'And you are Lily,' Chantelle acknowledged. 'The paparazzi's current must-have as Alessandro's new partner.'

'Friend,' Lily corrected.

'So shy, darling?'

As if to compound her words, Alessandro caught hold of Lily's hand and brought it to his lips. 'Lily is very beautiful, is she not?' His eyes gleamed as he looked deeply into her own.

'Exquisite,' Chantelle agreed. 'I hope she appreciates you.'

If he could play a part, then so would she. 'Alessandro is amazing. I am very fortunate to have him.'

Chantelle smiled and drifted into the crowd.

He leant in close. 'You haven't…'

'Had you yet?' Lily finished the sentence for him, and deliberately give him a stunning smile. 'And I never will.'

'So sure of that?'

She lifted a hand and cupped his jaw. 'Darling, of course I'm sure.'

It didn't help that he laughed, admittedly quietly, and didn't stray from her side for what remained of the evening.

In fact, she could almost swear his attention was meant to convey a *togetherness* he knew would annoy her.

At the witching hour of midnight the champagne flowed, toasts were gifted to their hosts, and an hour later a number of the guests had begun to disperse.

'Bed, I think,' Alessandro indicated, and Lily wrinkled her nose at him.

'Must we?'

'The party is all but over.'

So it was, but she was hesitant to be alone with him, even though the suite contained two beds. And although she was loath to admit it, she was tired. Working double shifts for the past few days was taking its toll.

It seemed expedient to capitulate, and she merely smiled as he gathered her close to his side.

She waited until they reached their suite and the door closed behind them before moving away from him.

'You can stop the pretence.'

One eyebrow arched. 'You think I am pretending?'

'Aren't you?'

He reached for her, and she gasped as he drew her close. Then his mouth was on hers, teasing, coaxing, *gentle,* in a way that was at variance with what she expected, and when she attempted to wrench free he merely framed her face as he traced the seam of her lips with the edge of his tongue, persuasive, tempting…and when she failed to comply, he opened his mouth over her own, nibbling a little as he tested the soft curve of her lower lip before taking its fullness between the edge of his teeth, easing it down to taste the soft inner tissue.

The temptation to nip him with the edge of her teeth was too great to deny...and she did. Or at least she tried, except light pressure on her jaw succeeded in allowing Alessandro the entry he sought.

Proof positive he possessed the strength to bend her to his will?

Instead he tasted, savouring gently in a kiss that melted her bones...or at least, that was what it felt like.

This was no power trip. Nor was it possession. Something more.

A promise.

Lily's mind reeled. *Dear heaven...promising what?*

Nothing she could want.

Nothing she dared need.

Liar.

If she kissed him back... Her mind screeched to a halt at the folly of giving in. *Madness.*

Complete and utter insanity.

Unbidden her hands reached for his shoulders, and pushed, wanting to be free of him. *Because she had to.*

As if he knew, he eased back a little, allowing her the freedom she sought as his hands shifted to cup her shoulders and he lifted his mouth from her own.

Lily could only look at him in stunned disbelief.

For a moment she seemed to have lost the power of rational speech, and she saw his eyes darken as he slid his hands to capture her head.

He smoothed a thumb over each cheek, dispelling the slow trickle of moisture, and her eyes widened in shock.

Tears?

She was *crying?*

She so rarely cried.

Not even in anger when she'd discovered James's infidelity.

An exception was the loss of her parents.

Yet Alessandro del Marco had tapped into her emotions and laid them bare.

It had to cease. *Here. Now.*

Lily opened her mouth to utter the words, except they were stalled as he pressed a finger to her lips.

'There is nothing you can say that will change what we just shared.'

She wanted to rail against him…and almost did.

Instead she moved away from him, gathered up her nightwear and retreated into the en suite, where she took her time with her nightly routine in the hope that when she emerged, he would be asleep in the bed…*his* bed.

Some hope.

Alessandro had retired to bed. Except he was awake, arms crossed above his head, and after an initial glance Lily ignored him completely as she crossed to *her* bed, slid between the covers, and settled down with her back to him.

Seconds later she heard the faint click of the lamp and the room was plunged into darkness.

'*Buona notte*, Liliana. Sleep well.'

Sure, and she could do that?

Except tiredness won out, and when she woke it was morning.

Coffee, she could smell coffee, and she lifted

her head, saw the carafe together with cup and saucer on the bedside table, together with a note, which she read.

With Giarda and Massimo. Join us when ready. Cruiser departs at eleven. A

Lily checked the time and immediately slid out from the bed, unable to believe she'd slept in so late.

Time to shower, dress in casual attire and head downstairs.

The cruiser proved to be in the luxury category, and twenty guests in all shared a catered brunch on board as Massimo took the wheel.

It was cool, with a brisk breeze, and Lily was glad she wore jeans and a woollen jumper, for there was a mist with the threat of rain.

Such a shame, although the guests made light of the weather, and the array of food provided for every preference. There was a never-ending supply of coffee, and Lily determined to enjoy herself, grateful as Alessandro pointed out points of interest, named each village and some of the history of the area.

He rarely moved from her side, and occasionally moved to stand behind her to direct her attention towards the Bocca di Angera as they passed by, the fishing village of Stresa, and Santa Caterina del Sasso Ballaro, which was built on rock and served as a monastery.

For some of the guests this was familiar territory, but Lily was fascinated by everything she saw, for it provided a different view from that gained by road.

It was easy to relax, to enjoy...and if there was conjecture about her relationship with Alessandro, she convinced herself she didn't care.

Massimo brought the cruiser in to berth mid-afternoon, and the remaining guests who had stayed over for the weekend began to slowly depart.

It had been delightful, and Lily said so as she thanked Giarda and Massimo for their hospitality.

The return trip to the city didn't seem to take as long, and it was pleasant to lean back against the headrest and let music from the disc-player take up the silence.

There was the temptation to close her eyes…
and perhaps she did for a short while.

It was early evening when Alessandro brought
the car to a halt outside her apartment, and she
thanked him as he accompanied her into the
lobby, then rode the lift with her to the third floor.

Outside the door of her apartment he drew her
close and covered her mouth with his own, then
he released her, took the keys from her hand,
unlocked the door, deposited her bag, and trailed
gentle fingers down her cheek.

'I'll call you.' Then he retraced his steps and
re-entered the lift.

Tomorrow she was rostered on for the early
shift, which meant an early start to the day.

CHAPTER ELEVEN

LILY slid into her car, fired the engine, and eased into traffic. The morning shift had involved few dramas, with the kitchen staff working in unison with efficient speed. Even Cristo displayed a remarkable lack of temperament, and the remainder of the afternoon stretched ahead offering a variety of options in which to occupy her time.

There was little urgency to make like a tourist, and browsing boutiques or department stores held little appeal. Food, on the other hand, held her interest, and she smiled at the thought of inspecting one of the city's better known delicatessens. Indulge in a specialty *latte,* select a few purchases, and when she was done she'd stop by a *gelato* bar and choose something delicious from the selection offered.

It was pleasant to examine the delicatessen wares, the large shaped jars with their preserved red, yellow and green capsicums; the bottled olives, sliced and roasted eggplant, the various salami, prosciutto, parma ham to mention a few. And the cheeses—so many to choose from. The display was akin to an Aladdin's cave of delicacies.

It was enough to make a seasoned gourmand salivate.

Lily made a small selection, paid, and collected a crisp crunchy bread roll. Dinner for one taken care of.

The gelato bar was next, where she chose a favourite, mango, and enjoyed every morsel.

It was almost dark when she reached her car, and after depositing her purchases onto the passenger seat she slid in behind the wheel.

Alessandro's image filled her mind as she engaged the engine. Admit it, he had become a constant, even when he wasn't physically present.

Examining *why* he affected her to such an emotional degree didn't supply any answers she was prepared to contemplate.

They didn't share a relationship per se. Yet it had become more than *friendship*. As to where it might lead...who knew?

Where do you want it to go? a silent voice taunted.

At that point her mind skittered away from the obvious. She could handle friendship, a few kisses, but taking the next step?

That was an entirely different ball game.

Although the thought of Alessandro in the role of *lover* held the power to liquefy her bones. Not to mention arouse every erogenous area in her body.

Don't go there.

She didn't need the heartache that would inevitably follow when the relationship came to an end.

Enough already.

Soon she'd be home, and there was the pleasure of a quiet evening alone. First she'd unpack her purchases, fix something light to eat, then she'd shower and relax.

With such thoughts in mind, she parked the car, gathered up her parcels, activated the remote locking mechanism, then she made her way to the apartment building.

The next instant a hard push from behind sent her sprawling to the ground, and for an instant shock robbed her of the ability to move, then she was scrambling to her feet.

Who...*why*? raced through her mind as she swung round towards her aggressor, and for a horrified second she saw only a man.

'Hello, Lily.'

Her vision sharpened at the sound of a familiar voice. *James?*

Lily's eyes widened in disbelief. 'What in *hell* do you think you're doing?'

'That should be *my* question, don't you think?'

He began moving towards her, and she stood her ground.

He cast the apartment building a sweeping glance. 'Nice digs, Lily. Rent must cost a bundle.' His gaze returned to spear her own. 'Is your new lover picking up the tab?'

None of this boded well, and she forced herself to remain calm. 'I pay my own way.'

'With your body?'

'I don't have to listen to this.'

'But I'm not done.'

'James...'

He took a step closer. 'Do you plead in his arms, Lily? Like it when he becomes...assertive, shall we say?' He jabbed a fist to her shoulder, and smiled as she steadied herself. *'Bitch.* You invite him in to your apartment. Go away with him for the weekend.'

He'd been *watching* her? The knowledge sent chills feathering her spine.

He slapped her face, and she reeled back in disbelief.

This was *James?* The seemingly placid man she'd almost married? Not once during their relationship had he been physically or verbally violent.

A little possessive on occasion, which at the time she'd considered protective. But *this*...this behaviour showed a side of him she could never have imagined he possessed.

Which only showed how well he'd played a part, and proved she really hadn't known him at all.

'You won't walk away from me.' He stepped forward and caught her shoulders in a punishing grip. Then he ground his mouth against her own.

Get away from him.

The words were a silent scream inside her head, and she lashed out with her foot, *hard,* and had the momentary satisfaction of hearing him grunt in pain.

His mouth on her own was a violation, and she bit his tongue in a bid to wrench free. For a brief second she thought she succeeded, except he was taller, heavier, and he had the advantage of anger.

The next instant his arm swung in a vicious arc to connect with the side of her head and sent her toppling to the ground.

Shocked pain vied with stunned disbelief. James...*James was attacking her?*

Something hard thudded painfully with her rib-cage, and like a wounded animal she screamed for help.

There was vague recollection of someone shouting, the sound of running footsteps, then an anxious male voice queried, 'Are you all right?'

Followed by a female voice... 'Are you hurt? Can you stand?'

Yes. Not sure.

Had she uttered the words aloud? Who knew? Her head didn't seem to be her own, and coherent thought wasn't really happening.

She was vaguely aware of a male voice in the

background, and she heard the words 'police', 'ambulance'…and began to protest.

'You need to see a doctor,' a female voice said gently. 'Is there anyone we can call for you?'

No. She moved tentatively…arms, legs OK. Sore head, sore ribs.

'My apartment building is just a few metres away.'

She caught sight of the bag containing her purchases lying in a mess of broken glass and seeping preservatives on the pavement.

'Here's your shoulder bag.' There was genuine regret in his voice as he indicated the bag of soiled food. 'Nothing to be saved there, I'm afraid.'

'We'll get you into the lobby and wait with you until help arrives,' the feminine voice assured.

She hurt most everywhere, and she could taste blood as she ran her tongue over her lower lip.

Wonderful. Just what she needed when she was rostered on to work the lunch and dinner shifts next day.

Maybe after a shower, some first aid, painkillers, she'd feel better in the morning.

'Thank you.'

It hurt to move, and she felt immensely grateful for the support offered as together the three of them made it slowly to the entrance. Lily punched the security code into the panel, the doors slid open, and she was helped into a chair.

She became vaguely aware of voices, the ding as lift doors opened, expressed concern…and the peal of a cell-phone.

The last thing she wanted was any fuss. In fact, all she wanted was the sanctuary of her apartment, a long hot shower, and to slip into her comfortable bed.

'I'll be fine to go to my apartment.'

'You've had a nasty experience,' someone soothed. 'It's probably best you rest quietly for a while.'

Five minutes, ten…then she'd *insist*.

Except she didn't get the opportunity as the entry doors slid open and a familiar male figure loomed large in the aperture.

Lily closed her eyes, then slowly opened them again as

Alessandro reached her side. She could try for humour or opt for silence… It was easier to choose the latter.

A muscle tensed at the edge of his jaw as he raked her pale features. *'Per meraviglia.'* The words were dangerously quiet as he crouched down in front of her.

'What are you doing here?'

Alessandro lifted a hand and gently tucked a lock of hair that had fallen onto her cheek behind her ear. 'The apartment manager rang me.'

'Why would he do that?'

'I own the building.'

Well, then. 'Why am I not surprised?'

He rose to his feet. 'Let's go.'

Hopefully up to her apartment, but caution had her querying, 'Go *where?*'

'A private medical centre.'

'I don't need—'

'Yes, you do.' He picked up her shoulder bag and carefully scooped her into his arms.

She cast him a cross look. 'I can walk.'

Not that he took any notice, and much to her chagrin he repeated the action when they reached the medical centre.

'There is no need for this.'

He didn't answer, merely settled her into a

chair in the waiting room and proceeded to take control.

A doctor examined her, organized blood tests, X-rays, scans, an injection…or was it two?

Lily lost count as an hour dragged by, then another before she was cleared to leave.

It didn't help her sense of modesty that Alessandro remained present during it all. Or that he took care of medical expenses, ignoring her protest without offering so much as a word.

Worse, it wasn't her apartment he returned her to, but his own.

'Why have you brought me here?' Lily demanded with exasperation as he cut the engine.

'I want to sleep nights,' Alessandro declared.

'So this…suggestion is entirely so you can rest easy?'

'Primarily your safety.'

'No.'

He, who ruled boardrooms with an iron fist, and never lost for a response, was somehow finding he was treading dangerous waters.

'You don't have the right to dictate to me,' Lily said, ignoring Alessandro's dark look.

'Caring for you gives me the right.'

'I didn't ask you to care.'

'Tough.'

This was fast approaching dangerous territory, a place she wasn't ready to visit just yet. For what seemed an age she simply looked at him, searching his features in an attempt to make sense of what remained unsaid.

'Choose, Lily,' Alessandro said quietly. 'My place or yours, but we share the same roof for as long as it takes.'

'Mine. Alone.'

'Madre di Dio. Must you be so stubborn?'

Stubborn didn't come close. Yet she was damned if she'd admit she was afraid...not of him, *herself.*

It was too much... He was too much.

'Take me home, Alessandro,' she said at last. 'Please,' she added. It was late, she was tired, wanting nothing more than a leisurely shower and to crawl into bed.

Lily almost expected him to refuse, or attempt to change her mind, and it came as a complete surprise when he ignited the engine and returned to her apartment.

She told herself she couldn't care less whether

he followed her indoors or not, nor would she admit to feeling immeasurably relieved when he did.

Without a further word she crossed to her bedroom, closed the door, then she shed her clothes and entered the en suite.

The hot pulsing water helped soothe tense muscles, and the combination of scented soap and steam felt good, so good, she stayed longer than necessary, emerging to towel off the moisture, brush out her hair and loosely plait it, before pulling on cotton sleep trousers, a sleep vest and emerging into the bedroom.

The apartment was quiet. She knew the front door was locked, yet a sense of self-preservation had her doing a final check.

It was then she caught a glimpse of a large male frame stretched out on a leather recliner chair in the lounge.

Alessandro. Minus shoes, jacket, tie. Asleep, if his steady breathing was any indication.

For a moment she wanted to shake him awake, then she heaved a deep sigh and retreated to the bedroom.

Surprisingly to sleep, and wake to the enticing

smell of freshly brewed coffee, toast, and, if she wasn't mistaken, bacon crisping in a pan.

Lily entered the kitchen to find Alessandro transferring bacon onto two plates, deftly following it with creamy scrambled eggs.

'*Buon giorno.*'

'I won't ask the obvious question.'

'Sit,' he commanded quietly. 'Eat.'

There was only one word she could summon. 'Bossy.'

'*Grazie.*'

'You can't stay here,' Lily voiced a trifle desperately.

He met her troubled gaze, and saw the doubt, the anguish and a trace of fear in her eyes.

Alessandro opted for a faintly wry smile. 'This chair isn't exactly comfortable.'

'Please, Alessandro.'

'Pack a bag while I call Giovanni.' He stood to his feet and stretched his arms high in an effort to ease the kinks in stiff muscles. 'Then you're coming with me.'

A frown creased her brow. 'I'm not going anywhere with you.'

'Yes, you are.' His voice held a hint of steel.

Lily huffed out an angry breath and spared him a dark look. 'You can't…'

'Easily,' he assured silkily. 'Whether you comply, or we do it the hard way.'

'I'm rostered on to work.' It was a desperate measure which had no effect whatsoever.

'As of now you're off the roster until such time as you're fit to return.'

'Says *who?*'

He took a step towards her, but refrained from touching her. 'I do.'

It was war as they went toe to toe, and at any other time they each might have glimpsed the humour in the stand-off.

Lily eyed him with fearless disregard, her eyes dark velvet brown brimming with speechless anger, while Alessandro continued to hold his ground.

The air between them sizzled with tension for several long seconds.

She wanted to refuse. Except she couldn't win. And her ribs, her head, *everything* ached too much to fight him.

'I don't like you.'

His mouth curved a little at the edges. 'Right at this moment, I don't expect you do.'

It didn't take long to retrieve a bag, add clothing and collect what else she needed before re-emerging into the lounge to deposit the bag at his feet.

Alessandro merely grasped the leather handles and hefted the bag over one shoulder. 'Don't forget your keys,' he reminded as he crossed the room to the door, leaving her to follow.

OK, so she'd made her point. Without a word she collected her laptop, then she covered the distance to the door, opened it, and summoned the lift.

The drive to Alessandro's apartment was achieved in silence, and the moment they were indoors she turned to face him.

'Happy, now?'

His eyes measured her own, deceptively calm, almost lazy in their regard. It was the faint hint of elemental ruthlessness just beneath the surface of his control that lifted her fine body hairs in instinctive self-defence.

'I'll go upstairs and unpack.'

She chose the guest suite she'd occupied when

both she and Sophia had stayed over following the Milan fashion after party.

There was a need to check the kitchen and see what she could prepare for their lunch. Both pantry and refrigerator were well-stocked and she sought Alessandro's home office, then she tapped the door twice.

There was no answer, and she knocked more forcibly.

Maybe he wasn't there.

Then the door opened and he stood in the aperture, looming far too tall since she'd ditched her heels for soft moccasins.

'Are you going to be here all day?'

'The prospect bothers you?' he queried evenly.

It bothered the *hell* out of her, but she was darned if she'd admit to it. 'Not at all. Will one o'clock suit you for lunch?'

For a second she thought she glimpsed a gleam of humour apparent, and her eyes sharpened a little.

'One o'clock will be fine.'

Lily inclined her head. 'I'd like to check my emails later. After lunch will be fine, if that's OK with you?'

On receiving his affirmative, she turned and retraced her steps to her suite.

Unaware Alessandro remained where he stood until she moved out of sight, before he thrust one hand in his trouser pocket and lifted the other to thread fingers through his hair.

He felt at odds with his emotions, alternately wanting to drag her into his arms and kiss her until she begged for mercy...or *what*?

Go one step further and take her to his bed? That would work...not. Bruised ribs, a narrow escape from concussion, add shock, and anything approaching intimacy wasn't going to happen. Yet.

Meanwhile, he had the distraction of work.

With lunch in mind, there was a need to decide what she should prepare.

Pasta was a staple, and there were sufficient fresh tomatoes, ingredients to make a basil pesto, bread rolls in the freezer she could use to make *bruschetta*.

It was pleasing to discover Alessandro had invested in excellent equipment, and for a kitchen in a private apartment it was a dream in which to work. Whoever drafted the plan *knew* where to build cupboards, place the dual ovens, the stove top, pull-out drawers in which to store saucepans. Plenty of bench space.

Did he cook? Or did he dine out?

At precisely one o'clock Lily put lunch on the table and tamped down a sudden jolt of nerves as Alessandro appeared without warning.

He possessed the silent tread of a cat, and for a second her hand shook as she indicated the table.

His eyes narrowed. Her features were pale, and bruising was beginning to appear around the twin butterfly strips at the edge of her forehead.

Silent anger rose to the surface against her ex-fiancé. It was only a matter of time before James's whereabouts were discovered.

He watched as she picked at her food, eating little before she pushed her plate aside.

'Not hungry?'

'I'm fine.' She stood up. 'You finish up while I make coffee.'

Alessandro let her go, and when he was done he entered the kitchen with crockery and utensils in his hand, deposited them on the bench.

'The pasta was superb,' he complimented as he collected his coffee. 'I'll take this with me.'

Lily merely inclined her head and continued stacking the dishwasher.

One night, she ruminated as she returned to her suite after logging her laptop to his Wi-Fi, then she'd return to her own apartment.

Something that she broached as they shared the kitchen clean-up following the evening meal.

'No.'

'What do you mean *no?*' Lily demanded. 'I'm perfectly fine.'

'James knows where you work, where you live. Until he's apprehended and charged, you will stay with me.'

'You have to be joking. That's ridiculous.'

'Tomorrow we'll head to my Lake Como villa for a few days. Mine,' he emphasized. 'As you know, James already has Sophia's address.'

Which successfully stalled the protest she wanted to voice.

James wouldn't…would he? A month ago she would have said no. But now? Who knew?

'As yet Sophia is unaware of the attack. Why distress her?'

It irked that he had a point.

'You're not giving me any options.'

Alessandro reached out and tucked back a stray lock of hair that had escaped the casual knot atop her head. 'No.'

He was close, much too close for comfort, and she silently cursed her quickened heartbeat as blood pulsed through her veins.

She wanted her life back, and a return to normality. Not an emotional see-saw that seemed to speed up with every passing day.

'I'm going to have an early night.'

Alessandro cupped her nape, saw her eyes dilate, and brushed his lips to her forehead. 'Sleep well.'

Something he wouldn't do, knowing she occupied a suite not too far from his own.

CHAPTER TWELVE

ALESSANDRO'S villa proved to be a luxurious mansion perched high on a hill above Lake Como, reached by a winding driveway lined with trees.

There was an air of tranquillity apparent, a sense of peace that permeated the beautifully appointed interior with its lush furniture and fittings. Exquisite lighting, ornate balustrades bracketing a wide curving staircase leading to an upper floor.

A mansion, but also a home, Lily decided as Alessandro assigned her a guest suite. It was, in a word, incredible. All of it. Sanctuary, she mused. Equally suitable for a pleasurable relaxed sojourn as it would be for entertaining.

'My housekeeper prepared lunch, and there's a lasagne in the refrigerator for dinner.' He placed her bag on a long chaise positioned adjacent a large window. 'There's a media room at the end of the hallway, and a library of DVDs. Feel free to explore the grounds if you choose.'

'Thank you.'

He had assumed a polite, but friendly *host* role, and that was perfectly fine. At least it provided a little distance, and that was a *good* thing, Lily conceded.

Not that she coveted his attention, or even his company. So *why* this vague feeling of disappointment? It hardly made any sense.

Admit it, she admonished as she unpacked her bag. *You like him. More than* like. *He stirs something deep inside you that you're afraid to explore.*

With every passing day it seems as if you are taking another step towards…*what?*

It would be so easy to give in, to enjoy sharing his bed, a part of his life, for as long as it took, no strings attached.

Maybe that was what she needed.

An affair.

Yet there was the knowledge that when it ended, she'd be broken-hearted and bereft, with little alternative but to leave Milan, Sophia, and settle far far away where she'd never see Alessandro again.

So why even take the first step down that path?

With the day stretching ahead, she connected to Alessandro's Internet connection, checked and answered emails, and after lunch she explored the manicured grounds.

The gardens bore hardy annuals, decorative shrubs perfectly shaped in unison, a functioning birdbath and to her delight the sight of a little black and white kitten sitting grooming itself in the weak sunshine.

'You adorable little thing.' She approached it with care, not wanting to frighten it away. 'I wonder who you belong to.' The kitten ceased its grooming and watched as Lily drew closer, tilting its head when Lily lowered down onto her knees.

Curious, the kitten padded forward, then stopped, before inching to within sniffing distance.

Lily slowly extended her hand, and after debating whether to risk moving closer the kitten bounded forward and almost fell over its front paws.

It was easy to scoop the tiny furry ball into her hands, and to Lily's amazement the kitten tucked its head into the curve of her palm and began to purr.

Love at first sight, and Lily lifted the little bundle and brushed it against her cheek and received a tentative lick in response.

From inside his home office Alessandro stood at the window and watched the scene play out. So the housekeeper's cat's new litter of kittens had reached the exploring stage, he mused, aware of the need to find homes for them soon.

Ah, there was Frederica, the mother cat, in search of her wayward offspring, and he saw the moment she sensed a human presence, her momentary struggle to pursue or retreat, only for the maternal instinct to win.

Would Lily hand the kitten over?

Gently she brushed her cheek against the little black bundle, then she carefully held the kitten in the palm of her hand and extended it for Frederica to examine.

The sweet gesture between two females, one human and the other animal, touched him in a way he was rarely affected, and he watched as

Lily allowed Frederica to attach her jaws to the kitten's neck, then trot back to where the rest of her brood were resting.

Knowing his housekeeper's soft heart, there was undoubtedly a soft blanket nestling in a basket somewhere safe.

He stood for several minutes as Lily rose to her feet and followed Frederica's progress until the cat disappeared from sight.

Dinner became a solitary meal as Alessandro was caught up with something obviously important requiring his presence in the office, and Lily ate alone, plated his lasagne ready to heat in the microwave, left a side salad with dressing and bread rolls under cover on the table, and sought the media room.

It was after ten when the movie she'd selected to watch came to an end, and she closed the unit down as the credits rolled.

Bed beckoned, and she entered her suite, shed her clothes, donned nightwear, then she completed her nightly routine and slid between the sheets of a very comfortable bed.

Sleep came easily, so too the disturbing images that brought her awake with a start. In the night's darkness she had a moment of not knowing where she was, until her memory engaged and the vivid replay of James's attack began to fade.

Not nice. Worse, no matter how she tried, any attempt to resume sleep proved elusive.

After what seemed an age she tossed aside the bedcovers and padded along the hallway to the head of the stairs.

Hot milk would help, and she eased her way down to the lobby, located the kitchen, heated milk in the microwave, then she moved to one of the French doors overlooking the gardens and sipped milk as her eyes became accustomed to the view.

It was there Alessandro found her, and he quietly said her name as he crossed to stand beside her.

Lily spared him a quick glance, glimpsed his bare chest, the jeans with the snap undone, and wondered what had disturbed *his* sleep.

'I'm so accustomed to working at full pace, the quieter life is affecting my sleep pattern,' she managed lightly, and hugged an arm across her midriff without being aware of doing so.

'No bad dreams?'

When she didn't answer he turned slightly and tilted her chin. 'Liliana?'

Why did he do that? She didn't need his gentle touch, or the soft huskiness in his voice. It affected her in a way she couldn't afford, heightening her senses to an alarming degree.

'Just one,' she admitted. *And I woke alone and didn't know where I was.* She held up the mug. 'Hot milk. Works every time.'

'Do you want to talk about it?'

Unbidden, a slight tremor shook her body. 'Not particularly.'

'Then let's get you back to bed.' Alessandro took the mug from her hand, placed it onto a small table, and caught hold of her hand.

She could almost believe the impossible, except to do so would be akin to chasing moonbeams. And she no longer had faith in fairy tales.

But one night, just one night in this man's arms would be heaven to her wounded soul. To feel wanted, even if it was only for a while. To fall asleep in warm arms, knowing when she woke he'd still be there.

Yet there would be the inevitable *afterwards,*

when, even if the sex was fantastic, it would be a one-off thing and where would that leave her?

So he'd escort her to her suite, then leave.

Except he didn't leave and she didn't tell him not to stay. One minute she stood looking at him, the next she heard a husky sound emerge from his throat as he moved into the bed and drew her down beside him.

'Sleep, Lily. And in the name of heaven don't move too much…there's only so much a man can take.'

It felt good. Better than good, and like the kitten she'd comforted earlier in the day, she tucked her head into the curve of his shoulder…and slept.

While he remained awake, fully aroused and aching.

Light was filtering through the shutters as she woke, and for a moment she thought she was back in her apartment. Except the room was wrong, the bed wasn't her own, and she was lying curled, spoon-fashion, into a warm male body.

Worse, a male hand cupped her breast.

A very aroused male.

'You're awake.'

'No, I'm sleeping and you're part of a very bad dream.'

She felt his warm breath against her hair, and she made an effort to free herself, without much success. And long after she had to wonder why she didn't put more effort into it.

Because she wanted what she shouldn't have?

A need to extend the comfort he offered?

Or because it felt *right* to remain exactly where she was?

All of it.

Yet she offered a token protest.

'I don't think this is a good idea.'

Alessandro lifted the weight of her hair aside and nuzzled the sensitive curve at the edge of her neck and her body trembled beneath his touch.

'You don't play fair,' she managed shakily, and gasped as he traced the curve with the edge of his tongue.

To give in, *succumb* to his ministrations, became an undeniable temptation, and a shaky sound left her lips as he traced a path low to the slight swell of her breast, then he gently bared it and took the sensitive peak into his mouth, savouring it as if it were the finest delicacy.

With the utmost care he slid both hands to catch the hem of her sleep vest and slowly eased it up over her head.

She met his dark slumbrous eyes, and was unable to look away as he shaped each breast and smoothed a thumb over each peak until they became tautly erect.

A faint gasp emerged from her throat as his hands slid to her waist, settled there, then his fingers sought the button fastening the elasticised waistband, freed it, then he smoothed the soft cotton over her thighs until the trousers pooled at her feet.

Instinct kicked in as she swiftly placed a protective hand over the soft curls shading her feminine core, only to have him cover it with his own.

'So shy, Liliana?'

A strangled gasp left her throat as he lowered his head and took her mouth with his own in a gentle exploratory kiss that blanked her mind to everything except *him*…his touch, the clean smell of soap he'd used in the shower mingling with the musky scent of man.

She was barely aware of his arm sliding down her back to cup her bottom as he urged her body in close against his own, making her achingly aware of the hard thickness of his erection.

Heat flooded her body as he sought the soft hair at the apex of her thighs and slid a finger between the damp folds, rested there, then he sought the acutely sensitive clitoris, felt her buck a little beneath his touch, only to sense her sharp indrawn breath as he skilfully brought her to orgasm, and held her as she shattered.

For long minutes she simply rested against him, too caught up with her body's reaction to move and she murmured an inaudible protest as he gently urged her to face him.

'Let me pleasure you.'

'You just did,' Lily managed in a voice husky with emotion, and heard his soft chuckle.

'Not enough,' Alessandro said quietly as he began trailing his mouth in a slow provocative path to the juncture of her thighs, parting them gently to lave the sweet moisture pooling there before probing the soft folds with his tongue, seeking and finding the engorged clitoris so acutely sensitive from his touch.

Ohmygod. Her fingers dug through the hair on his head and held on as he drove her wild, unaware of the guttural sounds emerging from her throat, or the way her body thrashed in the throes of ecstasy.

She became aware of a low keening cry and realized it was her own voice in protest as he paused momentarily to afford protection.

There was only one factor consuming every cell in her body: the need for his possession.

'Please...now.' The husky groan left her throat, and died to a whimper as he began a nibbling path over her stomach to pause at her breasts and gently bite the soft flesh there before taking possession of her mouth in a deep erotic kiss.

Just as she felt she could stand no more, he lifted his head and searched her passion-filled eyes with his own...and it was as if the earth stood still for a few timeless seconds, then he positioned his length and eased into her.

He saw her eyes dilate as she absorbed his size, and she arched her hips in silent encouragement. It was all he needed to plunge deep, and her lips parted with a soundless sigh as he began to move, slowly at first, then with increasing speed, taking her with him as he urged her high, so high she clung to him, so much a part of him as he took her to the brink, then he held her as she came apart.

She was beyond words, for she was at a loss to describe how she felt, or what she'd experienced in his arms.

Heaven. Simply heaven.

Later they shared a shower, and it was there she saw the faint white scars on his body; the tattoo on his left biceps, the small emblem at the edge of one hip.

Lily gently traced a scar, then another as she wondered what had occurred for him to receive them. Three were slashes from a knife. A puckered indentation defied identification.

'You find them repugnant?'

She met the darkness in his eyes, and slowly shook her head. 'No.' A lump rose in her throat and she swallowed it with difficulty. 'They're part of who you are.'

Without giving pause for thought, she leant in close and trailed each imperfection with her lips. 'Maybe one day you'll tell me about them.'

There was the need to crouch a little to trace the tattooed emblem at his hip, and she caught his indrawn breath as she rose to her feet and reached for him.

In one fluid movement she wound her thighs around his waist and brought his head down to her own as she sought his mouth in a provocative kiss that could only have one ending.

It was a while before they emerged to dry off, and even longer before Alessandro swept an arm beneath her thighs and carried her back to bed.

It was a few days later during dinner that Alessandro relayed the news that James had left Italy.

'How can you be so sure?' Lily said doubtfully, and glimpsed something dark and dangerously primitive in his eyes.

'I made him aware the threat of charges laid for stalking, his physical attack, would involve arrest and incarceration in an Italian prison,' he relayed silkily. 'Not to mention your intention to sue for documented injuries, deprivation of liberty.'

'You confronted him?' she said with disbelief, and glimpsed a muscle clench at the edge of his jaw.

'Did you imagine I would not?'

'Yes…no,' she said in confusion, and for a moment she didn't know what to say. 'That's it?'

Not quite, Alessandro reflected, although there was no need to relay everything.

'There's more?' Lily queried quietly, trying to read his expression, and failing miserably.

'If he values his skin, he'll drop his intended legal claim for compensation in any form from you.'

'You threatened him?'

'It depends on the interpretation of threat.' A reminder not to attempt to make contact with Lily at any time, under any circumstance.

The silence in the room grew.

'I see,' Lily said at last.

'What do you see?'

Too much…and not enough.

'I want to thank you,' she offered quietly. 'Your help and support have been invaluable.'

His eyes never left her own. '*Support,* Lily?'

It was fruitless to pretend when she retained such a vivid memory of precisely what they'd shared. In bed, and out of it.

He didn't move, yet she picked up on a subtle change…one that sent the nerves in her stomach on alert. There was a stillness apparent, a watchful element that hinted at control. His, reining in a silent anger that verged on the primitive.

'You've been very kind,' she added carefully. 'I owe you so much.' His presence since her arrival in Milan. His attendance as her social partner. Her position in his restaurant. Her apartment.

Oh, hell. Tell it how it *is*…gifting her something she didn't believe existed. *The beauty of unselfish loving.* Even thinking about what they'd shared sent the blood coursing through her veins, heating her body until it sang, vibrating with need… for him, only *him*.

Weeks…she'd only connected with Alessandro mere weeks ago. A friendship fostered by Sophia and granted from his affectionate loyalty to the caring couple who'd fashioned him into the man he'd become.

Yet it had progressed into *more* then mere friendship, Lily owned, reflecting on just how much *more*.

Was it real? Or simply a passing *convenient* flirtation that filled a gap in his life?

And how could she know?

She had little idea what drove her, other than an

instinctive need to discover if Alessandro was another *James*…a man who hid his true colours so well, she hadn't detected anything amiss during their relationship.

Trust needed to be earned and how could she be totally sure if she didn't test it?

'I think we each need some space.'

Alessandro's eyes darkened. 'Your reason being?'

There was a need to go on, now that she'd begun. 'I don't do casual relationships.'

'Is that what you think this is?'

She met his dark gaze fearlessly. 'Isn't it?'

'No.'

'Not just physical lust?'

'You consider physical lust to be a detriment?'

His voice was silky…almost dangerous. *No.* How could she, when her body came alive at the very thought of him…and *sang* with emotional reaction, as it did now, whenever his image filled her mind? As it did almost every waking minute of the day…and night.

It was madness, a madness she could ill afford if she wanted to retain a measure of common sense.

'Your body quivers with reaction every time I look at you,' Alessandro essayed quietly. 'The pulse at the base of your throat quickens its beat. You tremble at my touch, and when we make love, you gift me everything. Your heart...your soul.'

The unvarnished truth, yet she couldn't admit it. 'We have sex.'

'We make love,' he corrected, and saw her chin tilt in defiant bravado.

'There's a difference?'

If she imagined to make him angry, the attempt didn't succeed.

'That doesn't even qualify an answer.'

Lily indicated a gesture that encompassed them both. 'This—' she trailed, at a loss '—has hap- pened too fast.'

'And you consider that's a bad thing?'

Dear heaven. 'I had known James for almost a year before we became engaged. For months he shared my home, my bed,' she said with innate honesty. 'I believed he loved me...' She met his gaze with unwaveringly solemnity. 'As he's proven, I didn't know him at all.'

'You would compare me with him?' Alessandro demanded silkily.

Two men…as different as chalk from cheese. 'No.'

'Did you love him?

'I thought so.'

'Only *thought,* Liliana?'

Sensation spiralled through her body, as it always did when he chose to voice her birth name.

She searched his dark eyes in an attempt to determine something…*anything,* from his expression, and failed miserably. He'd had *years* of experience in acquiring an impenetrable mask, while she was an open book.

'James wanted an easy ride to what he perceived to be a charmed life. I was a young woman with a sizable inheritance, a successful business, a beautiful family home in an elite suburb.' She attempted a seemingly careless shrug. 'He played his part well.'

Alessandro resisted the need to pull her close and take her mouth with his own. There was more, and it needed to be dealt with before they could move forward.

'Is that what you think I'm doing?' he ventured quietly. 'Playing a part?'

Please, God...no. The touch of his mouth on her own, his hands on her body, the heart-wrenching emotions they both shared, the way she responded to him...and *his* response.

It couldn't be merely a practised act...could it?

He framed her face with his hands. 'My only need...is *you*. Everything you are. All of it. Your smile, the way your eyes light up when you look at me. The love you gift me with such generosity...' He lightly brushed her lips in a fleeting kiss. 'You take my breath away.'

The temptation to move in close, wind her arms around his neck and take his mouth with her own was uppermost...and she almost succumbed. *Almost.*

Her eyes held his...wide, fearless. 'What are you suggesting, Alessandro?'

'Sharing my life, my ring on your finger, the mother of the children I hope we'll have.'

Her mouth opened, but no sound emerged. Was it possible to be stunned into silence? Certainly at that precise moment there were no sensible words she could summon.

Marriage?

Lily swallowed the sudden lump that seemed to have risen in her throat. 'You can't be serious,' she managed at last, and glimpsed his slight smile.

'Liliana,' Alessandro chided gently, and glimpsed the soft tide of pink colour in her cheeks as he caught a host of vivid memories pass fleetingly across her expressive features.

Tangled limbs as they each sought to gift erotic pleasure to vulnerable curves and hollows. The soft intake of breath, the pent-up groan as sensual delight soared towards its peak. Hearts beating fast as they became lost in each other.

The sense of *rightness* in what they shared. The knowledge it could never be like this with anyone else...*ever.* Special, infinite.

'How can you make that kind of commitment after *so few weeks*?' she queried in a voice that held a mesh of shock and disbelief.

'Easily,' Alessandro stated, and watched her eyes flare with uncertainty.

Dear heaven. She needed time to get her head around this. Spontaneity was fine in some aspects of life...but *marriage*?

Yet there was a part of her that wanted to leap into his arms and say *yes*. To accept all he offered without thought or question.

She almost did…and knew he recognized the complexity of her emotions. Knew, on a subliminal level, that if he reached for her *now*, she'd be *his*.

Except, while he read her, he was also aware the next move had to be *hers*.

A consummate strategy, and a risk, but one he was willing to take.

'You have a week,' Alessandro said quietly, and saw her eyes coalesce from dark brown to almost ebony.

'And then?'

He took his time before responding. 'I'll come and get you.'

Ohmygod. The colour leeched from her cheeks, and, unbidden, the words tumbled forth without coherent thought. 'And if I choose to seek you out?'

His eyes speared her own, dark and impossibly unfathomable. 'You know how to find me.'

Yes, she did.

CHAPTER THIRTEEN

SLEEP proved elusive, and Lily rose next morning with the firm resolve to keep occupied, and work became a panacea as she beseeched the restaurant manager to allow her every shift available.

For four days and nights she worked tirelessly, taking only customary breaks, only to drive to her apartment, shower and fall into bed...then rise to do it all over again.

It didn't help. Nothing helped. And she still tossed and turned most of every night.

Each morning she recognized the ever-increasing dark circles beneath eyes heavy with lack of sleep, and used cosmetics to disguise them.

It was Hannah who took action in pulling Lily to one side at the end of an evening shift.

'Coffee. Then you tell me what the *hell* is going on with you.'

'I'm fine.'

'Uh-huh. Sure you are. There's a café a few doors down the street. Let's go.'

Seated, two *lattes* delivered to the table, Hannah pushed a container holding sugar tubes towards Lily, and leaned forward. 'Spill.'

'James has returned to Australia.' It was a place to start.

'Good riddance to a totally forgettable man.'

Amen to that.

'Alessandro?'

When Lily said nothing, Hannah pushed her *latte* to one side. 'The way he looks at you sends shivers down my spine. In a good way,' she added. 'What's the problem?'

Me, Lily admitted silently. *I'm the problem. Because I'm afraid to reach for the one thing I want. Apprehensive that I might be making a mistake. As I did with James.*

Yet with each waking hour it was becoming increasingly apparent how much she longed for Alessandro's touch. To feel his hands on her body, his mouth… *Oh, God.* She was becoming more of an emotional wreck with every passing day.

Even Sophia, when she telephoned, kept a silent

counsel, choosing not to mention Alessandro's name, and Lily had never felt so distressingly confused in her life.

Which was crazy. She could stop this emotional see-saw with one phone call.

So why don't you take control and do it?

'Nothing I can't handle,' Lily declared as she reached for her coffee, and sipped the delicious brew. 'Thanks.'

She bore Hannah's searching look, and offered a warm smile. The first genuine one she'd managed in days.

'Hey, did I just miss something here?'

'Not a thing,' she said gently, gathering her bag and extracting the necessary euros to cover their coffee. 'My treat. I insist.'

'You've made a decision,' Hannah essayed with satisfaction.

'Yes, I have.'

'Good.' Hannah collected her belongings and stood. 'Let's go.'

Together they walked to where their cars were parked, bade each other goodnight, then Lily fired the ignition and set the route leading to her apartment.

A shower worked wonders, and for the first time in several nights she slept like a baby, woke refreshed, and requested a change to the lunch shift in order to finish mid-afternoon.

Her plan was simple, and she chose her clothes carefully, worked the busy lunch shift, then drove to the stylish building housing Alessandro's suite of offices. Parking was a problem, and took longer than anticipated, causing concern as she rode a lift to the designated floor.

What if he was in a meeting? Consulting with an important client? Worse, what if he wasn't in his office at all?

The lift slid to a halt and she emerged into an elegant foyer, noted Del Marco Industries on a pair of wide glass doors directly in front of her, then she took a steadying breath and crossed into the stylish reception area where she was greeted with polite interest.

'Signor Alessandro del Marco,' Lily managed with equal politeness.

'Signor del Marco is in conference.'

'Could you inform his PA that Liliana Parisi wishes to speak with him when he's free?'

There was a flicker of recognition, momentary and easily missed if Lily hadn't chanced to catch it.

'Of course.' The receptionist turned to her console, pressed a button, spoke quietly, then deactivated the call. 'Christina will show you to Signor del Marco's private lounge.'

Within minutes a perfectly groomed young woman appeared, introduced herself, and bade Lily accompany her along a spacious hallway to a comfortably furnished room.

'Please take a seat. Signor del Marco will be with you soon. Can I offer you some refreshment? Coffee, tea…something cool?'

'Thank you. I'm fine.'

'There is a selection of magazines if you'd care to peruse them.'

It was easy to incline her head and proffer a smile.

Christina offered a compact electronic call device. 'If you need anything, don't hesitate to contact me.'

Then Lily was alone.

How *soon* was soon? Did it matter?

She'd skim through the pages of a magazine or

three, and attempt to ignore the onset of nerves playing havoc with her equilibrium.

The minutes crept by with seeming slowness as she turned page after page and barely registered a word or photograph.

One magazine, two and she was about to select a third when a door opened and Alessandro entered the lounge.

His eyes locked with her own as she rose to her feet and took a few steps towards him.

The look in his eyes almost brought her undone, and she offered him a tremulous smile as he crossed the lounge to meet her.

Alessandro didn't say a word, everything he felt for her was clearly evident. *Love,* in all its many facets, and caring.

For her...only her.

He lowered his head and brushed his lips to her own, felt their slight quiver, and lifted his hands to cradle her face.

For what seemed an age he savoured her mouth, tracing its outline, gently delving in to taste the sweet moistness as she met his persuasive tongue with her own.

Then she lifted her arms, linked her hands

behind his neck and held on as he deepened the kiss to something so incredibly passionate she lost sense of time and place.

For there was only the man, the strength of his powerful body imprinted against her own, the hard length of his arousal a potent force as he slid an arm down her back and held her close against the cradle of his hips.

It seemed an age before he eased the pressure and pressed his lips to the tip of her nose, her temple, then trailed light kisses along the edge of her jaw to gently tease the soft fullness of her lips before lifting his head a fraction to look deeply into her eyes.

'What took you so long?'

'Foolishness,' Lily owned, and ran the tip of her tongue over her swollen lips, saw his eyes flare, and she laid the palm of her hand against his cheek. 'Reasons I managed to convince myself were valid.'

'And they were not?'

It was time for honesty, with nothing withheld. 'I believed love needed time to grow from initial attraction to something…more. Not hit like a bolt of lightning and send my world spinning on its axis.'

Alessandro's mouth curved into a musing smile, parted, only for her to press his lips closed.

'After a disastrous relationship with James, I didn't want to have anything to do with men. But there you were,' she continued quietly. 'A constant in my life. At first I imagined it was out of a form of duty to Sophia. And I could appreciate that. Except it took an unexpected turn, and it was easy to confuse my emotions with good sex.' *Very* good sex, she amended silently. *Oh, go for broke...and accord it off the Richter scale.*

Lily paused, searching his features as she wordlessly begged him to understand.

'You think I didn't comprehend your uncertainty?' he queried gently.

Yes, he had, she perceived, setting the pace, not allowing it to stall. A superb strategist who knew her better than she knew herself.

'I love you.' Simple words that had been so difficult to recognize and accept, yet heartfelt and true.

'Grazie di Dio.' Husky emotion clouded his

voice as he claimed her mouth in a breathtaking kiss that rendered her breathless.

When he lifted his head, it was all she could do to look at him with tear-drenched eyes, and he smoothed a thumb gently beneath a lower lid where moisture threatened to spill.

'Liliana,' Alessandro chided gently as tears overflowed and tracked slowly down each cheek. 'You are my life.' He traced the twin rivulets and dispensed with them. 'You have my love. My heart.'

Lily wanted to cry and laugh, both at the same time. Instead, she lifted shaky fingers to each cheek, only to have him capture each and press his lips to the dampness.

'Let's get out of here, hmm?'

Lily offered a shaky smile. 'Are you done for the day?'

'The office…yes.' He pressed his mouth gently against her own. 'With you…no.' He curved an arm over her shoulders as he indicated the door.

Together they traversed the corridor, and as they reached Reception Alessandro extended a smile, acknowledged the receptionist and led Lily towards the bank of lifts.

When an electronic cubicle arrived he drew her inside, pressed the basement garage indicator, then he spared her a gleaming look as he lifted her hand to his lips.

If flesh and bones could melt, hers certainly *felt* as if they did.

This, everything she shared with this man was beyond price. All she could ever want.

It was true that occasionally fate chose to gift an opportunity. Something very special.

A gift she'd almost refused.

Because she couldn't conceive taking a leap of faith, *believing* what was in her heart…the very depths of her soul.

Alessandro's car rested in its reserved parking bay, and Lily took the passenger seat as Alessandro slid in behind the wheel.

Traffic was heavy, chaotic, and progress was slow, Consequently it took a while to reach the street that housed his apartment building, then he eased to a halt adjacent the main entrance.

Alessandro emerged from the car and crossed to where she stood, his eyes dark with passion as he drew her close.

'Thank you.' The words were slightly husky...
yet heartfelt.

'For what, specifically?' he probed gently.

'Everything,' Lily said simply. Caring. *Love.*

Nothing in his life held more meaning...
nothing except this woman who'd dispensed with
his seemingly impenetrable defences and taken
hold of his heart. As no other *could* in this lifetime.

There was little recollection who moved first,
only the fact his arms wrapped around her
slender form and his mouth took possession of
her own in a long hungry kiss that became all-
consuming, primitive, *urgent.*

Close, so close...the hard imprint of his body
melding with her own as they became lost in each
other. Aware of increasing need, and the desire
for more...so much *more.*

Skin on skin, the freedom to savour, suckle...
gift the ultimate in sensual pleasure.

Somehow she managed to pull back a little, and
a faint hiccup of laughter rose from her throat as
she bracketed his jaw with hands that shook a
little.

'We're standing in the street,' Lily offered quietly. 'Making out in plain sight.'

Dark eyes gleamed intently above her own. 'Not a good idea?'

He was teasing her, and she reciprocated by slowly running the tip of her tongue over her passion-swollen lower lip...and saw his eyes flare. 'I can think of a better one.' She pulled his head down to hers and whispered a few words in his ear.

Alessandro released a husky laugh in response, swept an arm beneath her thighs as he lifted her into his arms and strode to the front entrance, cleared Security and gained entry into the foyer.

'I'm perfectly capable of standing on my own two feet,' she chided as he summoned the lift.

In a matter of seconds the doors slid open, and he stepped inside, selected the appropriate number on the touch panel and the lift soared swiftly upward.

His lips nuzzled the soft curve of her neck. 'I'm interested in conserving your strength.'

She wanted to laugh and cry, both at the same time.

'Really?'

'Uh-huh.'

The lift eased to an electronic halt, the doors

slid open, and he crossed the hallway to his apartment.

Alessandro released the locking mechanism, stepped into the foyer, then closed the door behind them.

'You can put me down now.'

He pressed his mouth to her own, traced his tongue over the soft fullness as he continued through to the main bedroom.

It was then he allowed her to slide down to her feet, and his hands reached for her blouse, dealt with the buttons, then peeled it from her body.

The bra came next, and he cupped each breast, tested their slight weight, then he smoothed a thumb over each peak, caressing, stroking, until she moved restlessly beneath his touch, eager to dispense with his clothes as she freed his jacket, released his tie, then unbuttoned his shirt.

Next her fingers dealt with the belt fastening his trousers, released the zip fastening and whatever she might have said became lost as his mouth claimed hers in a kiss that took hold of her emotional heart and made it his own.

Lily retained no clear recollection of how the remainder of their clothing disappeared, there was only the awareness she was no longer standing, but lying in a tangle of limbs on soft sheets as Alessandro's wicked mouth delighted in gifting a sensual feast so intensely erotic it was almost more than she could bear.

There was a desperate need to reciprocate, and she pressed him onto his back, sent him a look filled with mysterious promise, then she sought the hollow at the base of his throat where a pulse thudded to a quickened beat.

Not content, she savoured there, teasing, suckling, nipping gently, before trailing soft kisses to one male hardened peak, then the other, where she rendered similar treatment.

His faint indrawn breath was an imperceptible sound as she slowly travelled to settle at his navel, exploring the indentation with exquisite care, drawing out his anticipation of precisely where her attention was aimed.

Smooth silky skin taut with desire, the swollen head a temptation she gently circled with the tip of her tongue, and heard him groan.

With soft kisses she traversed the hard length, teased a little, then trailed gently before gifting him the ultimate pleasure.

'Santo Cielo.' Words wrenched huskily from his throat, they were both benediction and oath as his powerful body trembled in a bid for control.

Lily's experience of feminine power was all too brief as his hands closed over her waist, and she found herself rolled beneath him in one fluid movement.

Then it became her turn to gasp as he surged into her and held steady while he fought to contain himself before he began to move, tantalizing her until it was she who begged for release in a voice she failed to recognize as her own.

Oh, dear heaven.

It was more, so much *more* than she believed possible. Mind and body in perfect accord with his own as they scaled the heights together, paused at the brink, then soared as acute sensation spiralled through their bodies in unison.

Eventually her rapid breathing slowed to something approaching normal, and she pressed her lips to his cheek, then his lips were on her own, gently, as he savoured the sweet sorcery that was hers alone.

She didn't want to move. Didn't think she *could.*

For a while they simply held each other in the exquisite aftermath of very good lovemaking.

Love, Lily amended as she dreamily reflected on the path her life had taken to this place, this man...and how, if not for fate, she might never have discovered either.

It was later, much later, that they rose from the bed, showered and donned casual clothes.

'I'll cook dinner,' Lily offered, and stood transfixed as Alessandro lifted a hand and trailed gentle fingers down her cheek.

'We'll do it together.'

The contents of his refrigerator and pantry presented numerous possibilities, and they fixed veal parmigiana, added a mixed salad, and a light chilled sauvignon blanc, finishing up with a delicious fruit sorbet.

It was as they sipped aromatic black coffee that Alessandro leaned forward and covered her hand with his own.

'Are you going to protest if I suggest we marry soon?'

Her eyes dilated a little. 'How soon is soon?'

'However long it takes to arrange a licence.'

* * *

Sophia's delight in their news was overwhelming, her excitement so genuine it almost brought Lily to tears as she became caught up with dress fittings, arranging to have the requisite documents couriered from Australia, a sizeable donation to the church in order for the local priest marry them in the privacy of Sophia's villa. No guests, just a small intimate family ceremony with the priest presiding.

'Please,' Lily appealed when Sophia protested. 'I cancelled the expensive wedding gown, the huge reception, the ornate cake planned for what became a fiasco.'

'I understand,' Sophia said gently. 'In that chase I shall organize a party on return from your honeymoon,' she enthused. 'It will be my gift to you both.'

'*Zia...*'

'You are my daughter before God, my beloved niece.'

Alessandro curved a gentle hand at Lily's nape. '*Grazie*, Sophia. We will accept with pleasure.'

* * *

Two weeks later Lily put the final touches to her make-up, her hair, and slid her feet into ivory stiletto heels.

The ivory silk gown was simply styled in elegant lines with a scooped neckline, three-quarter sleeves and a hemline swirling at her ankles. A fingertip veil fell from a delicate coronet of ivory silk rosebuds.

Jewellery was minimal, a diamond pendant on a fine platinum chain, matching ear-studs, and the beautiful diamond platinum ring Alessandro had gifted her.

With a smile that reached her eyes she turned towards her aunt.

'My darling Lily,' Sophia said gently. 'You look beautiful. I am so very happy for you.'

'Thank you. For everything,' she added in a voice husky with emotion as she caught her aunt close in an affectionate hug. 'Don't you dare cry. Or I'll cry with you, and then we'll both have to redo our make-up, which will make us late.' She moved back a step and smiled. 'Alessandro might think I've changed my mind.'

Sophia returned the smile with humour. 'I doubt he would allow it.'

No, he wouldn't. And the knowledge almost melted her bones.

'Alessandro loves you very much.'

'As I love him,' Lily said quietly. 'I didn't think it possible to love with all my heart. To know without a shred of doubt he is everything I could ever want or need. My life.'

'It was my hope, the focus of my prayers.'

She brushed her lips to Sophia's cheek, then she pressed light fingers to her aunt's mouth. 'Let's go, shall we?'

It was Sophia who would descend the staircase at Lily's side and accompany her to the formal lounge where Alessandro waited with the priest and Carlo as best man.

A very private intimate ceremony, followed by a celebratory meal, then they'd spend the night in Alessandro's Lake Como mansion before taking a flight the next day from Milan to Venice.

Venezia, with its arched bridges, canals, gondolas. *Magic*.

There wasn't a shred of doubt as Lily entered the lounge on Sophia's arm.

She saw Alessandro turn towards her, and for every day of the rest of her life she would never forget the look on his face as she walked towards him.

Love…in all its many facets, with the promise of undying passion. For her. Only her.

The depth of emotion apparent almost brought her undone, and she blinked in an effort to hold back the tears.

The room, its occupants faded from her vision as she saw only him, her smile soft and slightly tremulous as she reached his side.

Without a word she lifted her hands to cradle his face and kissed him, a fleeting soft touch of her mouth on his own, and so quietly only he could hear she said, 'I love you with all my heart. *Per sempre, amante.*'

For ever.

For the first time in his life Alessandro temporarily lost the power of speech, and he caught her hands in his own and brought them to his lips, his heart, his soul vividly reflected in his eyes as his mouth curved into a beautiful smile.

Later he would find the words…and show her with his body how much she meant to him.

Liliana. His life, the very air that he breathed. His one true love.

Per sempre.

* * * * *

Mills & Boon® Large Print
October 2011

PASSION AND THE PRINCE
Penny Jordan

FOR DUTY'S SAKE
Lucy Monroe

ALESSANDRO'S PRIZE
Helen Bianchin

MR AND MISCHIEF
Kate Hewitt

HER DESERT PRINCE
Rebecca Winters

THE BOSS'S SURPRISE SON
Teresa Carpenter

ORDINARY GIRL IN A TIARA
Jessica Hart

TEMPTED BY TROUBLE
Liz Fielding

Mills & Boon® Large Print
November 2011

THE MARRIAGE BETRAYAL
Lynne Graham

THE ICE PRINCE
Sandra Marton

DOUKAKIS'S APPRENTICE
Sarah Morgan

SURRENDER TO THE PAST
Carole Mortimer

HER OUTBACK COMMANDER
Margaret Way

A KISS TO SEAL THE DEAL
Nikki Logan

BABY ON THE RANCH
Susan Meier

GIRL IN A VINTAGE DRESS
Nicola Marsh

Mills & Boon® Online

Discover more romance at
www.millsandboon.co.uk

- **FREE** online reads
- **Books** up to one month before shops
- **Browse our books** before you buy

...and much more!

For exclusive competitions and instant updates:

 Like us on **facebook.com/romancehq**

 Follow us on **twitter.com/millsandboonuk**

Join us on **community.millsandboon.co.uk**

Visit us Online Sign up for our FREE eNewsletter at
www.millsandboon.co.uk